AURORA

a novel

ANDRE VLTCHEK

BADAK MERAH SEMESTA

2016

AURORA

Edited by: Tony Christini

Cover Art by: George Burchett

Cover Design by: Rossie Indira

Layout by: Rossie Indira

First edition, 2016

Published by PT. Badak Merah Semesta

Jl. Madrasah Azziyadah 16, Jakarta

http://badak-merah.weebly.com

email: badak.merah.press@gmail.com

ISBN: 978-602-73543-6-4

Jean-Paul Sartre, *Colonialism and Neocolonialism:*

"You know very well that we are exploiters. You know very well that we took the gold and the metals and then the oil of the 'new continents' and brought them back to the old mother countries. Not without excellent results: palaces, cathedrals, industrial capitals; and then whenever crisis threatened, the colonial markets were there to cushion or deflect it. Europe, stuffed with riches, granted *de jure* humanity to all its inhabitants: for us, a human being means 'accomplice,' since we have all benefited from colonial exploitation. This fat and pallid continent has ended up lapsing into what Fanon rightly calls 'narcissism.' Cocteau was irritated by Paris, 'the city which is always talking about itself.' What else is Europe doing? Or that super-European monster, North America? What empty chatter: liberty, equality, fraternity, love, honour, country and who knows what else?"

Eduardo Galeano, *Open Veins of Latin America*:

"You could build a silver bridge from Potosí to Madrid from what was mined here – and one back with the bones of those that died taking it out."

Andre Vltchek

by the same author

Exposing Lies of the Empire
Fighting Against Western Imperialism
On Western Terrorism: From Hiroshima to Drone
Warfare (with Noam Chomsky)
The World Order and Revolution! (with
Christopher Black & Peter Koenig)
Western Terror: From Potosi to Baghdad
Indonesia: Archipelago of Fear
Exile (with Pramoedya Ananta Toer & Rossie
Indira)
Oceania – Neocolonialism, Nukes & Bones

Fiction:
Point of No Return
Nalezeny
Plays: 'Ghosts of Valparaiso' and 'Conversations
with James'

Andre Vltchek

PART - I
Encounters

Andre Vltchek

1

Mozart And Brecht In Valparaiso

And

Introducing Hans G

At dusk, Bertolt Brecht and Wolfgang Amadeus Mozart entered an ancient tango bar in the old Chilean port city of Valparaiso. At that hour, Cafe Cinzano remained nearly empty. A shy if ardent middle-age couple held hands at a distant table and whispered sweet words over tall glasses of foamy pisco sour. An enormous, fat orange cat stretched comfortably on the floor, certain that, as happened every day, it would feast before long on copious leftovers of fish and seafood.

"*Tell me about your trip to Southeast Asia.*"
Brecht put his hand on Mozart's shoulder.

They ordered white wine and a basket of
empanadas filled with prawns.

"*Pablo Orozco was accompanying his wife,
Aurora, back to her native land. They went for
a one-week visit. And I joined them. There,
they met a man, a director of a major
European cultural institution...*"

"*...Who turned out to be an intelligence
agent?*"

"*How did you know?*" Mozart opened his
mouth, pretending to be shocked.

"*Most of them are, aren't they?*"

"*Many years ago he was involved in the
murder of Aurora's younger sister.*"

"*Tell me everything,*" insisted Brecht. "*I
love her work. Aurora is one of my favorite
artists, a real revolutionary. And her husband,
Pablo Orozco is also one of the people I
genuinely admire.*"

"*We all do,*" nodded Mozart. "*But say: do
you really want to hear everything, from the
beginning to the end?*"

"*Yes, please, right from the start.*"

"*But Bertolt, I warn you, it is a strange,
complex and dark story.*"

They raised glasses to each other's health.

"*I'm glad we've met again, Wolfgang. Last
time we talked was in Caracas.*"

"*Yes, it was two years ago. And before that,
in Beijing – just one year earlier.*"

"*When Comrades Shostakovich and Victor
Hugo joined us.*"

"Precisely. But now, let me begin the story. I am eager to share with you what took place in that faraway and unfortunate country."

Nauseatingly sweet smoke from clove cigarettes swirled into fantastic forms. Ghostlike, the smoke filtered through the dimly visible tropical vegetation and levitated into the starless night sky. The outdoor café in one of the country's former capitals once again overflowed with local artists, all uniformly dressed in dark-colored T-shirts, jeans and plastic sandals, their grimy feet resting on old chair frames and worn-out cushions. Their faces, detached and mildly cynical. The few women wore clothes identical to their male companions, and they too smoked clove cigarettes. In the semi-darkness, the women were difficult to distinguish from the men. All seemed desperate to blend into the obscurity of the night.

This nation of thousands of islands and languages once proud of its diversity had descended into gray uniformity – its cities and villages increasingly indistinguishable one from another. People were worn down. So many dressed in the same untidy and unattractive fashion, behaving the same way, believing in the same things, thinking alike, submitting to the same religions, to capitalism and to repressive family structures. Differences had not been tolerated for many decades. Independence was broken at an early age, considered dangerous and evil.

Mozart: Like in my old Vienna.
Brecht: Like in all parts of the world where
oppressive cultures reign.

Hans G, a European cultural envoy in this "far away land," sat at one of the rough and robust wooden tables in the center of the café, his disciples surrounding him, something truly ancient and biblical in the gathering. Other men and women were gathered there for no particular reason, perhaps simply savoring the honor of being seen engaged in a sophisticated conversation with such an important man of culture.

Hans felt at home in this café and in this ancient city. He also felt at home in the appalling, polluted and hopelessly overcrowded national capital, a few hundred kilometers away. In fact he felt at home everywhere in the enormous country cushioned by deep tropical greenery, surrounded by seas and oceans, dotted with tremendous volcanoes that had a tendency to explode at the most unexpected moments, spitting out deadly lava. To Hans, it mattered very little that most of the trees were logged out and that the seas and rivers were hopelessly polluted. Should even the volcanoes grow indignant and be determined to confront and punish humans for remorselessly devastating the entire archipelago, this would matter not at all to Hans.

As far as Hans was concerned, the country consisted of countless "mysterious indigenous cultures," of peculiar subdued tropical sounds, of slow, hesitant movements and gestures of local people, and of countless masks covering the faces of both adults and children. Masks were everywhere, especially glued onto the faces of politicians and hangers-on, hiding emotions, joy and pain, truth and fabrications.

This was a country that had undergone unimaginable suffering. Memories of terror bled continuously from past to present and pooled in the houses and villages across the country.

On the isles of this archipelago at night no stories of the past were told, even inside close family circles. Eyes were averted from so much, from one another, very few questions were asked.

Hans liked this perpetual silence. He seemed to savor the people's fear.

For him, to be simply there at that table in that café was an indispensable part of his mission. He liked what he did. He worked hard. He never complained though there were countless tasks assigned. By now he spoke the local language - not too well but well enough to understand some nuance, to establish and maintain important contacts, and to secure desirable outcomes.

In various parts of Asia, Hans was very famous, or, some would say, notorious. It was a well known fact that he could easily make or break almost any artist and intellectual living on the archipelago. He could fly him or preferably her to Europe, after arranging an exhibition, a speaking assignment or a film screening. He could effortlessly create coverage or set up an interview with major European corporate media. Most importantly, he could fund and therefore control any promising project, while guiding it in any direction he considered appropriate, stripping it of any left-wing ideological elements.

In this once revolutionary but now stagnant and feudal land, power was greatly appreciated and widely recognized as the most desirable and respected quality a man could possess. Hans had been enjoying his power to the fullest in a land where an esteemed and influential man was a man who was secure, safe, all but untouchable. At the level that Hans operated, there was absolutely no danger of being confronted, criticized or insulted, let alone dethroned from his pleasures and power. There was no risk of being humiliated, or exposed. Humiliation and disgrace were those conditions strictly reserved for the poor majority. Hans enjoyed the fullest support and protection of his own mighty European nation, of the West in general, and of the regime that governed the entire archipelago on behalf of the West.

It mattered very little how such power had been attained. Only power itself was important. Power guaranteed the essential and the delightful: immunity from attack and the obedience or total submission of others.

A genocidal but well-positioned and strongly-backed General in this land, as in many lands, was always feared, admired, obeyed. Should he be elevated to President, nobody would blink or dare criticize his past. A mendacious priest stealing from his congregation was venerated, so long as he could flash and command wealth. Thieves posing as businessmen were respected the more they looted, the more they flaunted fancy watches, expensive cars, extravagant mansions.

Brecht: Naturally, they learned all this from us – from Europe.

Mozart: No doubt about that, Bertolt, no doubt! However, in Europe, corruption and theft were elevated to a cynical but almost elegant form of high art. Where Aurora comes from, a once elegant and ancient culture was reduced to absolute vulgarity, by the European colonizers.

Brecht: We of the West insist that even the quality of corruption be greater than the corruption standards of our lessers.

Mozart: Making us the kind of teachers who both teach and thwart our students so as to stillbirth any challenge.

Brecht: For grimly do we reap as we sow.

Mozart: It's biblical with a twist, I agree.

For a man in his mid sixties – for Hans G – power was also about buying time, at least twenty extra years, maybe more. It meant turning the clock back dramatically. Women and their curves were almost all that Hans G lived for. Local people, mostly women, whom

Hans G funded as well as those who dreamed of being funded by him, were at all times ready to overlook his wrinkles and fleeing hairline and make him believe that it was Hans and only Hans they were interested in, Hans and not the prestigious art projects that he manufactured and managed. Local women knew a thing or two about the vanity of powerful males. Some had become absolute virtuosos, playing the egos of the powerful as if they were Stradivarius violins. The art of tickling the masculine narcissism of power had been developed and perfected during long centuries of colonialism and the parallel period of local feudalism. Now in the era of savage capitalism this art had been modified and refined, reaching near perfection. Women with their slow elegant gestures, with big, seductive, revolving eyes and slender feet offered their bodies, their flattering words and tenderness to any ruler, arch-thief, CEO, military strongman, Mafioso, or any high-flying preacher or imam, in exchange for protection and mercantile favors. This brutal archipelago continued to be one of the most volatile and dangerous places on earth, particularly for women. A terrible, almost animalistic fear and uncertainty turned even some of the purest into courtesans. Behind the various masks worn by men hid the lowest desires. Rape and extortion were as frequent and pervasive as the mighty downpours of rain. This was how it had been for centuries, with the one exception of a short revolutionary period that ended in a horrendous bloodbath fomented by the West.

But for a powerful man like Hans, for a man who liked women more than anything else on earth, this country offered limitless opportunities to sample the delightful fruits of Eden.

After working here for several years, Hans had forgotten – or tried to convince himself that he had forgotten – the depressing rot that ravaged his own continent. He tried to forget about the endless cold rainfalls of northern Europe, the fog and empty streets after sunset, the burning loneliness and late night despair. He knew perfectly well that it was unimaginable for him to return to the West. He did not want to suffer at night the pain of solitude as he had done for so many years before coming to Asia. He did not want to relive the drinking sprees in half-empty pubs and bars. He did not want to feel irrelevant, unwanted, disposable. Here, he was a demigod. Back home, he was a boring, aging fool.

When he read in the newspapers that hundreds of the elderly had died in Paris during the latest heat wave – abandoned and alone, helpless – he swore he would not go back to Europe to face what the Japanese call the 'lonely death.' He could not bear to endure the long years, possibly decades, staring at mossy walls and red flowerpots outside his windows from the nowhere of his bedroom. He refused his useless memories. He did not want a venomous solitude. He dreaded the idea of owning a dog or a cat in a medieval central

European city. He did not want to go to impersonal bordellos to buy a few smiles and a bit of pathetic tenderness. What he wanted was all here: being surrounded by real people, admiring people, preferably people much younger than himself – people at his mercy, people full of energy, and narcissist hopes and selfish dreams about their futures, corruptible people, go-getters, egotistic and pragmatic, anyone who might be oh so fully aware of the significance of being associated with such an important figure as himself.

Hans after all was a man of the people who could elevate dozens of his disciples to the great heights of stardom, as easily as he could break the spines of countless rebels unwilling to collaborate. He dispersed the money of the regime. He did not have to pay from his own pocket for any of the favors he provided. What an arrangement! Especially considering that the beneficiaries showed their gratitude directly and personally to him. They felt obliged to him. The regime was simply too big, and too abstract, somewhere beyond the horizon. It was all but impossible to identify and lick the regime's ass. But Hans was right there, right next to them, ready to receive their caresses, their flattering words, their tenderness and passion. Real or phony, he did not care, as long as it felt good and could last forever.

Of course the regime and its structures were repulsive. Hans and the other foot soldiers of Empire made sure this fact remained concealed. Sometimes he suffered terrible nightmares, imagining the system as an enormous decaying fish, tossed on the seashore by a tidal wave. He recalled "The Tin Drum," "La Dolce Vita" and many other films containing similar disturbing images. He did not want to be part of the monstrous, putrefying body that he was ordered and paid to promote, a body he had faithfully served for decades, the cold, rigid body he simultaneously despised and worshipped, now at a distance, and belonged to so fully – the body of Europe and its culture.

Hans' existential dilemmas vanished almost as soon as they appeared. Though Hans was something of a thinking man's propagandist – sensitive, artistic – he was most of all realistic. The pleasure he received from local liaisons was constant and unending, silencing all doubts.

He served his government and his culture well from afar. He was remunerated and offered many rewards and benefits. Further down the chain, he remunerated those willing to collaborate with the system through him personally. He was fully aware of his role in destroying the land and culture of the people in whose submissive embraces and fake caresses he found comfort, security, a second home and even his second youth. The pleasure of being in charge, the pleasure of giving orders, as well as those boundless physical pleasures that he experienced almost every night, were so intoxicating as to reliably silence almost all negative thoughts and emotions.

Brecht: Sad, endlessly sad. The only decent thing would be if he'd find some courage and blow his damned brains out.

Mozart: European joys, occasional sadness, a murderer's tears... They rape and kill, then they feel melancholic, if not thrilled. All that matters: their egos and gonads.

Brecht: He knows... Do you think he knows that he comes from shit and that he is driving that poor Asian country to even greater shit?

Mozart: At least subconsciously, he knows.

Brecht: A long time ago, I wrote a poem. A short poem:

> *I sit by the roadside*
> *The driver changes the wheel.*
> *I do not like the place from which I have come.*
> *I do not like the place I am going to.*
> *Why with impatience do I*
> *Watch him change the wheel?*

Right now Hans was blissfully happy, and that was all that mattered, even if happiness came in spasms, lasting only a short while, a few hours at a time.

The young men and women surrounding him in this open-air café were so courteous, overflowing with compliments, politely smiling at him, fixing their eyes religiously on his lips as he continued to benevolently reply to their fiery declarations and timid requests. They laughed when he made clumsy, even idiotic German jokes. He had no illusions about his own wit and sense of humor. He knew he was dull, mediocre, thoroughly predictable. His smiles looked like the grimaces of a martyr, painful to watch. But he paid regally for the solidarity and benevolence of others, for his followers making him feel special, brilliant, ingenious. They laughed even when they couldn't understand the true meaning of his words. They laughed instinctively, as do all good lackeys and courtesans. They screwed their faces in compassionate grimaces when he spoke half-heartedly about poverty and other big, serious issues.

He had learned how to chat fluently about uncomfortable and controversial topics. He had learned while on countless assignments in Asian countries. Poverty had to be mentioned at least once in a while, or so his supervisors explained to him during his training. Poverty was always a good subject, as long as the discussion remained superficial. "Poverty has to be handled lightly and with special care, because it is like dynamite," he was told on several occasions. It should never be politicized. He used poverty, corruption and education as topics designated for 'breaking the ice.' Naturally he didn't give a flying fuck about poverty here or in any other country of the world, including his own. Thanks to that very poverty, people like him were able to feel good, superior, rich and in charge. Thanks to poverty and under-development, good jobs for people like Hans were always available. Thanks to poverty, elites could thrive, feel special and be different from the rest, the filthy and ignorant masses. One can only feel really good and unique about being rich when most everyone else is eating shit and drinking stale piss. He was also perfectly well aware that his young listeners were unconcerned about poverty in their country: they were educated to be self-centered and merciless. They danced and giggled inside glass and steel malls, with direct views of open gutters clogged with filth and dead rats, where children suffering from malnutrition swam and played. He was the one who had carefully selected them – he needed such people. It was not difficult to find appropriate candidates. It was always form over substance. That was what he preached to them, indirectly sometimes, but persistently. And that was what the West had taught everyone everywhere, for many decades. Art was never supposed to be about ideas. The purpose of art was not to bring transformation. For God's sake, it was not to trigger a damned revolution. Art mainly existed in order to entertain. Art was for searching inside the tiny egoistic souls of the artists, to tickle their egos, and of course to decorate empty spaces. Art had been converted into a submissive craft, used by the rich, the corrupt to beautify their mansions. The wilder the colors and forms on the canvases, the easier it was to say: this country is free, even if there were no ideas, no rebellion, no statements mixed in with the pathetic shallow madness and extravaganza. A few exposed female breasts in a gallery, and the West could describe its creation – the entire oppressed archipelago – as 'progressive' and 'tolerant.'

One of the greatest revolutionary novels ever written, Hugo's *Les Misérables*, was known here only as a Broadway musical, to which local elites flocked during weekend trips to Singapore.

Pollock and Warhol were promoted as the giants of art, as unquestionable role models and eternal inspiration.

Hans kept recalling those words written a long time ago by Frances Stonor Saunders, for *The Independent*:

"For decades in art circles it was either a rumour or a joke, but now it is confirmed as a fact. The Central Intelligence Agency used American modern art – including the works of such artists as Jackson Pollock, Robert Motherwell, Willem de Kooning and Mark Rothko – as a weapon in the Cold War. In the manner of a Renaissance prince – except that it acted secretly – the CIA fostered and promoted American Abstract Expressionist painting around the world for more than 20 years."

Hans loved the expression "in the manner of a Renaissance prince." It was he, he, and he! The prince was he – an aristocrat and warrior against those left wing plebes and degenerates.

All this was happening even now, or

especially now. If not supported directly by the CIA, then by countless Western "cultural institutions," including the one that Hans led.

Hans and many people like Hans worked day and night, making sure that art never became truly politically or ideologically engaged, that it never dared to address the most essential issues humanity faced. This was the main purpose for his existence, the single most important part of the mission – his claim to fame. He had plenty of allies and limitless ammunition available – an entire system of grants, elaborate funding mechanisms, lavish scholarship schemes, as well as a great army of owners and curators of all sorts of commercial galleries. He could count on collaborative and obedient editors and writers warming chairs at corporate media outlets, publishing houses, and most university presses. His allies were based in the West and across the Asian continent. Here, they were embedded into virtually all islands of the archipelago – infiltrating the government, religious institutions and the corporate world, even the military.

Thinking about his work and great achievements, Hans G began smiling cheerfully. And as he showed his uneven teeth, dozens of young people who had been courting him and fighting for his attention, smiled back in unison. They had no idea why he had decided to grin, they did not know why they were beaming back, but they felt, intuitively, that it was exactly what was expected of them.

And they were right.

'Whores!' whispered Hans under his breath. 'You spineless pieces of shit! How much I love you. Especially those of you with big boobs and cunts wide open for my thick, superior Aryan tool!'

The world was undoubtedly a good place, according to Hans. It was clearly very good to him, and to hundreds of thousands of men and women like him. The rest be, of course, damned!

Throughout evenings like this one, he felt alive, secure, content and proud. He felt almost euphoric. Before coming to this part of the world he had never experienced such outbursts of raw excitement. He would murder millions, without blinking an eye, if that was the price of preserving this ecstasy, this powerful romantic drumming inside his chest. Yes, he was truly a romantic man: an extraordinary being in extreme and extraordinary circumstances.

Brecht: An extraordinary swine.

Mozart: In an extraordinarily filthy gutter...

Andre Vltchek

2

Aurora Enters The Stage. Suddenly It Is Dawn Everywhere

Mozart: Then the monster's eyes rested on her...

Then he saw her, first noticing a ravishing silhouette, slow movements and her feline, confident and elegant walk. A simple but perfectly cut knee-length dress hiding and at the same time exaggerating her beautiful curves, and fragile body held so upright, resting on the marvelous architecture of her feet in simple open black sandals. Her long jet-black hair fell naturally down, covering her shoulders.

She was advancing, walking towards him,

her captivating black round eyes fixed on his face.

This was the middle of the night, but all of a sudden it felt as if there were a new dawn in this desperate place packed with morons and covered in smoke. For Hans, it would be dawn now for all time, as far as he could see.

He thought he had died for a few seconds and immediately thereafter experienced rebirth, a resurrection. The planet had altered its orbit. The earth moved. Hans was traversing the sun now in a way he knew he had never known before.

Brecht: How tacky! Hemingway: "For Whom The Bell Tolls." What a great novel, and a great quote. But not coming from the mouth of that arch-pig!

Mozart: I know... I read his mind. That is exactly what he was mumbling. The earth moved...

He closed his eyes and opened them again and there she stood in front of him. He stood to face her, to welcome her into his life – her head meeting the level of his shoulders only despite her heels and perfect erect posture. He extended his hand. He took in her intoxicating gentle scent that made its way through the cloying stench of the clove smoke.

Then she spoke, her voice deep and silky and fatal. She talked to him. She did not utter many words. She addressed him and he listened to her voice without trying to understand the meaning. When he started to comprehend what she was saying, a cold shiver ran down his body. He shook, mortified.

"What are you doing to my country?" she asked, slowly, piercing him with her deep black eyes. "What the hell are you doing to my poor land, you dirty spy, you agent, you subhuman filth?"

Mozart: I was truly impressed by how precisely she captured the essence. "Sotto humano," we would say in a libretto.

Brecht: A few more things could have been added, but the essence was definitely captured.

Andre Vltchek

3

Filth And More Filth On Hans G

*H*ans G. always held his heavy Aryan head high. He felt proud of his sizable skull adorned with close-cut graying hair, proud of his shaved Nordic face with black-framed spectacles, proud of the whiteness of his skin. But these were only details, important, but details nevertheless. More important was his lofty status, his being the man selected to represent the greatest and triumphant (European) culture in the enormous, chaotic and filthy capital of one of the most vast and most miserable countries on Earth. What a responsibility! What an extraordinary and heroic calling! Hans felt this was a gigantic, almost Wagnerian, task. He was convinced that he brought light to a space consumed by absolute darkness, that he enlightened at least a few selected individuals in a nation that had lost its brains and almost all of its creativity.

Was he manipulating reality? So what? He was instilling foreign values, and his values were undeniably superior! In this pitiful country where he was based, there were no permanent theaters left, no concert halls to speak of, and only a handful of cinemas showing pathetic second-rate Hollywood rubbish alongside an indigestible medley of Southeast Asian horror movies. The Cultural Center that he was in charge of was a true shining jewel in the crown of the Empire's artistic grandeur. It was undeniably one of a very few places in the capital that was still truly dedicated to 'real art.' Hans made sure that it hosted at least a few international musicians every year, that it showed artsy films and staged exhibitions of local painters and sculptors. Free wine was served at the openings. Some women wore high heels, and he had spotted one or two neckties during a recent concert. For him, his work and his position, it was nothing less than a modern-day cultural crusade, and a labor of love.

That was his official story: 'How Hans must perceive Hans,' so to speak.

Things were, naturally, much more complicated.

Upon any close examination, the Center's activities were nothing more than high-level entertainment for the local 'elites.' Hans was well aware of the fact that the upper class of the capital city was badly brought-up, uneducated, and hopelessly vulgar. Men and women who were part of that exclusive group could not actually take more than fifteen minutes of Chopin, nor ten minutes without checking their phones. When in the Center's restaurant, they habitually licked their forks. Like the rest of the people in the country, they suffered from a chronic lack of concentration. Generally they did not give a flying fuck about Western high art. They frequented the Center in order to be seen, to underline their uniqueness, definitely not to learn about Mahler or Schumann. Some of them came hoping to meet foreigners, to feel that they were like them, or to get laid, to catch a husband or a wife, a lover or a patron. Hans had to cater to the tastes of local 'elites.' A program too refined would offend them. A concert 'too complex' would leave the hall half-empty after the intermission.

This was the true, unofficial side of the story: 'Hans both manipulated and served local elites.'

Then, there was a secret that captured perhaps the most revealing thing: 'He actually despised them all.'

Brecht: Plus the ideological part of it...
Mozart: I'm getting there...

No revolutionary ideas were allowed to penetrate the walls of the Center, nothing containing a dose of socialist or (god forbid!) Communist ideology had ever been exhibited or performed there. The reality of the world presented by Hans to 'the locals' was meticulously simplified, stripped of all deeper thoughts and uncomfortable details. Thinking had been discouraged for decades. Nobody cared about any damned 'deep thoughts.' Hans knew it. It was to his advantage. He was not here to teach reason, on the contrary! As a result, the Center offered countless 'light' concerts of Western classical music, as well as depoliticized art exhibitions and a complete menu of local traditional dances. Hans loved traditional dances – they were colorful and safe. He adored when the women knelt and rolled their eyes, while twisting slender fingers. Such performances pleased everyone.

And Hans was eager to please. He did not want anything 'negative,' disturbing, or controversial to resonate in his cultural kingdom! Definitely nothing political that could annoy or god-forbid threaten the local fascist regime. At the Center, he never allowed anything that shed light on the several brutal ongoing genocides the regime committed in the occupied islands so rich in minerals and timber, islands plundered on behalf of powerful multi-national mining and logging conglomerates.

There were no moral dilemmas that haunted Hans at night. He was a European man, serving his continent. He was doing what had to be done, in order for the civilized part of the world to retain full control of the Planet. Overall, he felt proud and content.

For many years, Hans bore two major and closely interlinked responsibilities: first, to preside over the Cultural Center; second, to head the duty station of his country's intelligence agency. Both activities he found to be intellectually demanding, even tiring.

Making things more complicated, after the 'events' of September 11, he had been ordered to accelerate all information sharing and to cooperate directly and closely with the Americans, Brits, French, Dutch and Australians. For decades and centuries, these five nations had intensively engaged in Southeast Asia, their activities ranging from directly colonizing entire countries and regions, to overthrowing unsuitable governments, supporting fundamentalist pro-market regimes and, at the softer end, spreading all types of anti-Chinese, anti-Russian and anti-Communist propaganda. Under their omnipresent and watchful eyes and leadership, corruption and extremist religious activities thrived, while left wing and nationalist movements were systematically liquidated.

Hans perceived himself to be an artist. His tragedy was that no one else really considered him as such. As far as his colleagues and handlers were concerned, he was a reliable and professional demagogue and propagandist – actually an excellent demagogue and propagandist, a real virtuoso, but nothing more than that. His main duty was to ensure that this nightmarish land was constantly glorified at home and abroad. All client states of the West had to be praised, relentlessly. Criticism had to be suppressed by any means, well, necessary. And public opinion the world over had to be constantly massaged and manipulated. Creating a positive image of this archipelago was of utmost importance. The more undemocratic or outright fascist and feudal was the allied country, the more it need to be promoted as a sprawling democracy. The more its minorities trembled in fear, the more 'tolerant and accepting' must Western corporate media plug such lands. Flowery praise at diplomatic receptions and during state visits was standard. The genocides committed here were hardly ever mentioned in Europe and North America. Such trifling details did not matter. Who would, at least in London, Berlin and Washington, be interested in criticizing a regime that diligently robbed tens of millions of its own citizens to feed the West, and to sustain its selfish gluttony? Who in the West would ever dream of attacking a system that had managed to fully enslave its nation, after breaking it and turning its people into tens of millions of submissive buffalos (to borrow the provocative and desperate words of one of the last living Communist artists of this land). The buffalos were by now unable to imagine any better world. The buffalos constantly demanded more capitalism and more religion and more Western pop, and more plunder of their own natural resources, as well as more enslavement and family despotism. The buffalos voluntarily marched towards the bloody and horrific slaughterhouse.

'Culture always plays an extremely important role in forming the nation.' Hans was constantly paraphrasing someone whose name he could not recall. Was it Marx, Lenin, Jan Amos Comenius? Who cared? It was true.

The buffalos seemed to have fallen in love with their own idiocy. Actually, they had no idea that their idiocy was truly an idiocy. They did not understand that their fear was fear. They were oblivious to the fact that their country was thoroughly covered in shit, that it was fucked to no end. They were like so many people in every land. And that was good. It was brilliant that they did not see the world, their world, for what it was. That was how it was meant to be. Hans G worked hard, day and night, to make sure that things continued this way. He was succeeding. And that was one of the main reasons why he held his heavy Aryan head so high. He was brilliant and powerful. He could both see and manipulate what others could not, dared not, or would not.

*

It was understood that prostituted local elites should be pampered, made to feel exceptional. It had to be done sensitively, since typically they suffered from a complex of inferiority. They had to be guided and provided with a cultural home and a new identity. Elites did not want to be associated with their barbaric nation. They needed something higher, something that could clearly separate them from the uneducated, dirty and boorish masses. The masses were pissing and shitting into canals, and boiling food in the same water. The more detached from their people the 'elites' became, the more eagerly and faithfully they served the Empire. Some subscribed to *The Economist*, listened to the *Voice of America*, gave each other names like Michael and Deborah, became fundamentalist preachers and ran exclusive Christian private schools. The more Western the better. Their intellectually, morally and emotionally debauched offspring, 'the future of the nation,' had to be taken into account as well: lazy, selfish, and ignorant but ambitious young men and women were given scholarships and sent to various schools in Europe, Australia, Japan and the United States, where, not surprisingly, they found it relatively easy to fit in. Naturally Hans was in charge of this highly effective project too.

He knew that local 'elites' were always ready to commit high treason – which is what they had been doing for decades and centuries – in exchange for power and feudal privileges given to them by foreign rulers. However, even the protocol – how the treason should be committed – had to be carefully planned and controlled by people like Hans. Nothing could be too obvious. Whoring had to be wrapped in the national flags, passed off as patriotism.

Ideological and economic collaboration brought Ferraris and Range Rovers to the streets of the capital, and paid for hundreds of thousands of square meters of marble and granite floors in the grotesquely extravagant boutiques, malls, golf clubs and hotels. Money came easy, so huge amounts of cash were tossed around aimlessly and without a second thought.

The servile mass media kept its mouth shut, as did the local writers and artists. Hans was in charge of "creative people," not the press. Several of his colleagues from various countries and agencies handled the media.

By now, the system functioned flawlessly. There were no ideological and rational attacks against the regime. The country produced almost nothing, invented nothing, and apart from timber, minerals, oil and textiles exported close to nothing. Deep in intellectual stupor, it was unable to give birth to even one respected scientist, critical thinker, artist or reformer. And it didn't seem to give a damn. Knowledge and resistance had lost their importance and luster decades ago. They were made irrelevant, described as boring and outdated. Local brains were conditioned to accept unbridled corruption, to concentrate on consumption, and to question nothing.

Hans made sure that while the elites were supplied with a few musicals as well as extremely small doses of Mozart and Bach (but mostly Anglo, local and K-pop), the cheapest and most vulgar local and imported entertainment was pushed down the throats of the oblivious, some would even say lobotomized, masses.

*

A conservative Cold War warrior and true European nationalist at heart (yes, he now perceived Europe to be a single nation), Hans G believed in using a heavy hand when dealing with the locals. Democracy had to be promoted. And democracy was basically "what the West decides that it should be." It was essential that superior Western values were spread and upheld. To achieve that, undesirable local elements had to be kept at bay. Hans did not do this the way it was habitually done in Central and South America, in the Middle East, in Africa and even in some parts of Asia by agents of various Western countries. Under his supervision, no children were raped in front of their parents, no villages were directly sprayed with deadly chemicals, no depleted uranium was used, and very few public figures were assassinated in broad daylight. Some still were, but not many, and Hans was not the one who gave the direct commands. He was not responsible for electrodes attached to the balls, vaginas and nipples of local dissidents (not that there were many dissidents left in this country), for tubes with starving rats inserted into female genitals, for prisoners being thrown from flying helicopters. Some colleagues operating in other parts of the world had used all of these anti-subversion methods in the past and in some places they were still doing it. But Hans could proudly testify that this was not his "*Spiel*". There was no need for it. The local military, paramilitary and police were doing all the torturing, raping, assassinating and blackmailing of their own people. Of course almost all the heads of these institutions were trained in the West – in North America, Europe and Australia – where they were taught how to terrorize and keep at bay their own population. But by now, local security forces did not need any foreign assistance. They had become almost perfect, their work flawless. The country was now excelling at least in one area – brutality. As a result, people like Hans could keep their conscience clean: they became bureaucrats, theoretical planners or even creative figures. The bottom line was that Hans left all the violent and filthy work to his local counterparts, while concentrating on what he knew how to twist and manipulate the best, in fact with unmatchable brilliance – the culture. He personally did not have to get dirty.

Mozart: But he did get dirty, from time to time. Just a tiny bit – a few corpses here and there, a few violated women...

Brecht: Worlds collide, statistical error, entitled excess...

The archipelago was now exactly where Europe and North America wanted it to be.

Brecht: That is, deep in the rectum...

Naturally, even now, some violence and "persuasive techniques" needed to be periodically used by foreign superintendents like Hans. Though the zeal of the local cadres was indisputable, their brainpower was not. There were occasions when one had to intervene on the spur of the moment and take action, particularly when some adversary suddenly become too smart, too dangerous, too effective. After all, no capitalist wanted to take risks here, in this country overflowing with raw materials and cheap obedient labor. This was not Laos. This was an enormous modern-day Potosi!

*

Decades ago, millions of local people had perished, here, where the West had performed an enormous, daring and thorough experiment. First it helped to overthrow the progressive nationalist government and then it ordered the local military and religious cadres to go on a rampage and perpetrate an unimaginable orgy of terror. The goal was to observe and to study how a once proud and revolutionary nation would react to being bathed in blood, the indescribable horrors of genocide. How would it behave if it were to be suddenly chained, tortured, humiliated and then covered and choked by a thick putrid blanket of fear? Would it resist? Would it fall to its knees? Would it beg? Would it rise? Would it become submissive? The West's logic was simple: better to kill millions of people than to allow some potentially rich and patriotic Asian country to continue marching on a socialist path, to allow it to vote democratically for aligning with the Soviet Union or Communist China. In the end, here, an extremely complex and yet simple model was born, then developed and perfected. This model would be later copied and freely implemented all over the world, in such diverse places as Chile, Rwanda and the former Soviet Union.

Information about these events had to be wholly distorted. The West helped the local regime ideologically, teaching its rulers the essentials about propaganda. Victims were described as perpetrators, mass murderers as heroes. End of story! Communism was banned. Atheism was banned. Religion made obligatory. An entire nation was converted into something resembling the German Nazi Protestant enclave in the south of Chile during Pinochet's dictatorship: *Colonia Dignidad*.

Before the coup, European Protestant preachers were sent to the major cities of the archipelago where they went to work, indoctrinating, corrupting, training and preparing Christian, Muslim, and even Hindu cadres for the upcoming massive onslaught against the "atheists." Soon they were joined by thousands of Chinese émigrés, mostly protestant preachers and regressive members of the lower middle class, people who had only recently fled from the Chinese Revolution and now were ready to collaborate with any anti-Communist project, no matter how surreal or brutal. They were put in charge of the massive brainwashing and deception campaign, both ideological and religious. After the coup they were strongly encouraged to snitch, to deliver local patriots to the dungeons, and into the claws of torturers and executioners. Among them were Protestant preachers, now aging members of the local 'elites,' living inside gated communities, driven by chauffeurs, their ailments treated in private clinics. This was their idea of 'freedom' after leaving revolutionary China.

The United States, Europe and Australia masterminded, triggered and then sponsored the entire bloodbath that lasted for months. Their agents helped to identify and murder the most patriotic, anti-imperialist and left-leaning citizens. The embassy of the United States supplied the local military with a long list of those who had to be liquidated. But the local assassins were so intoxicated by blood and the screams of their victims that they ended up killing 3 million people instead of several thousand. Women from progressive organizations were gang raped, and then their breasts were cut off, publicly. Men were forced to dig their own graves before being bayonetted and thrown into the deep pits. Countless intellectuals and teachers were imprisoned or slaughtered. The West assisted the murderers while indoctrinating the local population with capitalist and anti-Communist dogmas. The culture was not spared. Traditional theaters were shut down, stages burned to ash, film studios destroyed, books torched.

Rivers were clogged with corpses.

The era of darkness had begun.

Hans and others made sure that all of those horrors were erased from the memory of the nation. Things had to become blurry. No books addressing the past were to be written, no films with substantial budgets were produced and shown, no exhibitions staged.

It all happened many years ago, and Hans sincerely and benevolently believed that at the present time there was no urgent need for such extreme brutality. The system functioned by inertia, smoothly and almost flawlessly. People were too passive and uneducated to harbor lofty revolutionary ideas. They were conditioned into believing that the way they lived was near perfect. Each local leader was on the payroll of either a foreign business conglomerate or a government (or both). Communism had been crushed and was banned. Religion had become obligatory and the law made it illegal to criticize it publicly. No political force ready to defend the nation's dispossessed, miserable and ignorant majority was left anywhere on the entire archipelago. Case closed!

Hans and his colleagues made sure that here the People's Republic of China was smeared, depicted as a brutal enemy and a new super-capitalist empire, not as the tremendously resourceful Communist nation that it largely was, a country that had been standing, together with Russia, Latin America and others, against Western imperialism. All local newspapers regularly reprinted Western anti-Chinese propaganda pieces. Russia too was demonized in countless editorials, documentaries and "news pieces," translated from English to several local languages. All Latin American revolutions were ridiculed through propaganda skillfully interwoven into the culture. A basic unanimity was achieved and maintained. It was founded on ignorance, brewed in far-away capitals, and it was extremely effective.

Hans liked to think that he and his Machiavellian brilliance were at least partly responsible for the roaring success of the ideological onslaught.

*

Americans did most of the direct arm-twisting, at least when a forceful approach was still required. Europeans took care of the gentler aspects like planning, ideology, propaganda and cultural indoctrination.

As far as Hans was concerned, in 'his line of work,' there was no immediate need for electric shocks, 'submarines,' waterboarding and poisons. His main weapons consisted of exhibition spaces, choirs, grants, direct funding and press conferences. His old chums like Beethoven and Mozart, as well as several 'newer' ones like Warhol and Pollock, provided the best cover for the operations.

Mozart: This is what that imbecile was really thinking!

Brecht: How could you tolerate such a disgrace, Wolfgang?

Mozart: I poisoned him on several occasions, with a laxative. I was planning to do much more, soon...

Andre Vltchek

4

The Regime Rewards Hans G Who Was Now Regularly Sodomizing Rina In Front Of Mozart

*H*ans' reputation in the high circles of the regime rose steadily. His rewards were plentiful: an enormous villa with a tropical garden and a swimming pool in the best neighborhood of the capital, a chauffeur-driven limousine, several attractive maids, a passable cook and an odd gardener who was known for having conversations with snails. Financial allowances were generous as well.

When it came to women, Hans G always aimed high. Modesty was unnecessary. Even now when he was well over sixty, he felt no need to lower himself with bar girls or secretaries. He could afford the best, and this year the best came in the fantastic shape and color of the most famous local filmmaker – Rina – a woman with a slim, sublime body, who had shocked the nation with her socially charged films spiced with sexually explicit scenes and gutter language. As with almost all local artists at some point in their lives, Rina discovered that she needed a patron – a 'big man' who would be able to 'connect her' to the moneyed world outside this culturally and geographically isolated intellectual and artistic backwater. And no local artist could have the slightest doubt that for these tasks Hans G was the most suitable 'big man' in town.

Two years ago Rina had approached him. They spoke, drank wine, and negotiated. He proposed to her, offering several options. She demanded more, much more. Eventually, they reached a mutually acceptable compromise. No more films with social messages – that was one of his principal conditions. And then, starting from the evening when the unwritten agreement was reached, it was understood that her body would exclusively belong to him.

Now Rina's films were fully funded from abroad. Two of them received prestigious international awards and enthusiastic reviews. One film told a story of growing up in an idyllic village somewhere lost in time and deep in the countryside. It was not easy to find a place where the film could be shot, as the appalling misery, filth and deprivation scarred almost the entire archipelago. Bad tongues had said, although it was never confirmed, that all scenes related to crystal-clear creeks cutting through the countryside were actually filmed in Malaysia. The other film was about the dazzling business success of a once poor and handicapped woman. At the end of the second film, the heroine drove her newly acquired Porsche Carrera on a narrow country road. She wore Armani sunglasses, while loudly and merrily singing *I did it my way*.

Rina seemed to pretend to care: "With you, I sacrificed my talent and my conscience. Now my films are pure rubbish. Wherever I go, I feel ashamed! I avoid the eyes of people on the street. I feel like an intellectual whore. And to you I gave up my precious body!" This is what Rina often shouted at Hans. Then she would usually add, wryly: "You'd better pay me well for all this!"

And he did.

He would sometimes remind her: "You came to me first. Never forget that it was you who actually teased me and gave me your body."

While never managing to fully control Rina's mind, Hans G had at least completely conquered her curves. He took full advantage of his 'rights.' His favorite late-night activity was brutal: it consisted of turning her forcefully onto her stomach, face down and buried in one of his *Zara Home* pillows. He then dropped on top of her, using his robust physique against her fragility. Almost every night they spent together, he fucked her in the ass to hurt her, using no lubricant, contemplating her moaning, savoring her pain, closely observing her small delightful dark body twisting and thrashing from left to right in agony, making a beautiful color contrast on the snow-white sheets. In the morning, after the pain and humiliation, she would threaten to leave him, again and again, but he knew she was incapable of making that move – not so soon, not as long as the invitations continued to arrive from Vienna, Zurich and Berlin, not as long as the prestigious institutions offered to show her films, not for as long as the funding flowed from his cultural institute directly into her swelling bank accounts, not for as long as... She would not dare to leave him while he was 'in charge of the culture' in this part of the world. The well-paid intellectual whores never abandoned the really big men like him. For years and decades to come, she would be at his mercy, and they both knew it, just as they both knew that her situation and her physical position and contortions during their endless nights together were not unlike those of her entire nation in relation to Hans G.

For as long as she willingly or unwillingly remained on her stomach, buttocks in the air, exposed, defenseless, for as long as she kept her commitment to not make any socially conscious films at home or abroad, Hans would support her work, and provide for her increasingly lavish lifestyle.

While Rina cried in pain, the confused and indignant eyes of Wolfgang Amadeus Mozart, whose portrait hung on the wall above the bed, stared at Hans, sadly, accusingly.

"What a piece of shit you are, Hans G!" Mozart's eyes declared, while Hans thrust his Viagra-enhanced Nordic weapon into the rectum of the tearful subservient film director. "*Du bist aber Schwein!*"

"You were not always a saint yourself, Wolfgang Amadeus," replied Hans in his mind, as wordless, they often communicated.

Mozart's eyes seemed to have the incredible ability to read his mind and to communicate answers. "Of course, of course," his eyes would say, sadly. "I was never a saint. In my days, no one in Vienna, Berlin or Prague was anywhere near sainthood. But this is something else – this is extreme, something absolutely repulsive and unpardonable: an anus for patronage! An anus for art! *Ein Arsch – für die Kunst!* So to speak."

Hans liked that. He would move with greater and greater speed. He pounded and salivated like a dog. "*Ein Arsch – für die Kunst!*" He fell in love instantly with the phrase. "*Ein Arsch – für die Kunst! Ein Arsch – für die Kunst! Ja ja ja!!!*" he chanted mentally, a maniac.

He grabbed the long jet-black hair of the filmmaker, and pulled at it forcefully. He kept pulling and pulling, while the artist beneath him screamed.

"*Schwein,*" frowned Mozart. "You pig."

"*Ja!*" Hans glared point-blank at Mozart before suddenly ejaculating into his victim. For a moment he was as breathless as the wretch beneath him. Then: "Mozart, you dog, it feels good to be on top and in control, no? And not only does it feel good, it is nothing less than a tribute to our great culture!"

Hans knew that his joke was absolutely tasteless and awfully Germanic ... if one could even call it a joke. But he could not help making it. He felt like the master of the universe.

In the face of the absolutely abhorrent, the composer of *Don Giovanni* could find no suitable reply.

Brecht: Does he always know when you are watching?

Mozart: No, he is never certain. I am actually very rarely there. He knows that I periodically check on him, but he is not sure when. He is not even sure that I am what I really am. Sometimes I talk. When I do, he thinks he is dreaming, that I am an insignificant nightmare, not a ghost.

Brecht: It is all truly appalling. But in a way, he is correct: he really represents the essence of European culture: to serve and to rape, to lie, to dictate and to indoctrinate. Die Kunst...

Mozart: Yes, die Kunst.

Brecht: Die Kunst – oh that filthy whore!

5

Hans G Is Enchanted With Aurora. But Then...

"*P*lease sit down," he addressed her. His voice sounded formal even to him, unnatural.

She ignored his invitation, still standing in front of him, erect, confident and cold.

Feeling her wrath, he began perspiring. Was it fear? All of a sudden things felt unsettling and humiliating. Sticky torrents of sweat drenched his custom-made *batik* shirt. When in this country he always wore exquisite, locally tailored batik chemises, preferably of dark, somber colors. His Hugo Boss trousers and batik tops always matched surprisingly well, a unique fusion of one of the world-renowned German designers with a centuries old tradition of local garment making. Respect for local cultures had to be shown continuously. He was advised and trained to always, well, at least on the surface, to appear reverential, to promote and glorify everything related to local customs and culture.

But sweat now painted new and unexpected designs on his fine shirt, and soon he worried these were dark and uneven patterns of shame.

He looked around. He knew that his disciples heard and registered every word. They always listened attentively. They sometimes pretended they did not, but he was certain they were all ears.

"How much are they paying you?" she asked in her even and terrifying tone of voice. No hysteria, no high-pitched notes. Rather, perfectly balanced, composed speech, flavored with tiny needles of spite.

Suddenly he felt unwell. She had begun to drive long and sharp nails deep into his body. His bowels were ready to move, right then and there. He was uncertain, not knowing what would come next. Firm and perfectly choreographed encounters were essential to his work. No surprises, no improvisations could be allowed, which could collapse the entire elaborate structure. Her appearance here was not part of any good script. It astonished him. It disarmed him. It made him vulnerable.

"Calm down," he said, but then immediately realized the absurdity of his own words. She was absolutely calm, while he was perspiring and beginning to shake.

There was no fear in her eyes. He was not used to that. The people he encountered in this country were always petrified. Almost all. They were scared of something concrete or abstract, or both, but they were profoundly frightened. That was how things were supposed to work here. It was planned. Fear was essential. Fear was instilled in into people at birth. Hans knew that he, his partners and all of their local allies could only operate and thrive in an atmosphere of absolute fear.

This entire nation was scared of something, day and night. The nation was so accustomed to fear that most of the people inhabiting it were not even aware, anymore, of the fact that they were chronically terrified. To experience constant fear was normal, a regular state of mind. Fear and submission were commonly confused with morality or obedience, which amounted to the same thing here, and, strangely, with love: love of the country, obedience to the economic system, love of religion, obedience to the law, love of family, obedience to the rulers. Obedience to country, religion, and family. Love of the economic system, love of the law, love of the rulers. Obey. Love and obey, or else. You feared what you loved, and vice versa. You loved and you feared. Submission and obedience had become synonymous with love, as common in fanatical and brutal Protestant sects.

People like Hans G were feared, but they were also scared of other people, as they were of so many things. They were scared secretly of those whom they controlled, and of those whose lives they ruined. The more frightened they were, the taller more protective the walls they erected around themselves, the more firmly in charge they had to be.

To Hans, a lack of fear in someone's eyes was unacceptable. It was actually terrifying, clear proof that he was failing in his mission and an unmistakable sign that he himself was facing mortal danger.

"Do they pay you a flat retainer or do you get remunerated one per person, a per capita basis, for every person that you corrupt, silence and destroy? Or what is really the arrangement?"

Brecht: Good question!

Mozart: Yes, very good. I actually found out: he gets a monthly salary as a regular office clerk, and also a package of benefits and fat bonuses, here and there, depending on his performance.

"Who are you?" he wondered.
"My name is Aurora."

Brecht: What style our Aurora has.
Mozart: Yes, what style!

6

Pablo Orozco Enters The Stage

*T*hen Hans G noticed the tall, commanding figure of a man sitting at a nearby table. He knew instantly, almost intuitively, who that man was, and his feeling of invincibility shrunk ever further. In fact it was almost smashed to pieces. He felt dizzy. His feeling of unease kept mounting. A sticky sweat now covered his entire body, leaving large dark spots on his shirt and trousers.

How could this be happening? Why hadn't he, Hans G, a man 'in charge of culture,' been alerted beforehand? How was it possible that this dangerous foreigner had not been stopped at the airport, the seaport, wherever he had entered the country?

Hans recognized Pablo Orozco, one of the

living symbols of the Venezuelan Revolution.

A 'dangerous foreigner,' Pablo Orozco, was now sitting comfortably on a cracked and stained chair, in this damned filthy dive full of fucked-up, untalented, lazy and thoroughly prostituted local scribes and artistes. Why the hell had he come here, to this laboratory that had been, until now, so perfectly managed by Hans G? What terrible luck, what an insane coincidence! Why did it happen? No accomplished outsiders ever came here! No great artist, no great thinker bothered to visit this brain-dead archipelago, especially this motherfucking degenerate town. This country was for second-rate businessmen and aging sexual tourists. It had been cut off from the rest of the world, on purpose, for decades! It was supposed to be completely isolated and quarantined! That had been the plan, since the mid 1960s. So why this, why now? What was one of the greatest, and at the same time one of the most provocative artists on Earth, doing in this intellectual bordello?

When Hans spotted him, Orozco was not calling for rebellion in art and philosophy. He was not telling how, in his studio in Caracas, he was splashing red paint all over his massive canvases. Instead, his enormous hands were making simple *origami* for two street children that he had insisted be allowed to enter this café with him and Aurora. One child on each knee, Orozco fashioned tiny paper cranes and other fabulous creatures, talking to the children in Spanish, English and in broken local language.

For a grand figure of the Latin American Revolution, for a guru of engaged, combative art, for a symbol of everything that Hans was laboriously and tirelessly trying to disappear and keep disappeared in this part of the world, Orozco looked surprisingly simple, even timid. There was not a trace of arrogance or superiority engraved on his face. He was merely enjoying his quiet interaction with the children, talking and drinking beer.

'And the most troubling thing is,' thought Hans, 'there is no trace of fear in Orozco's face.'

Hans remembered that he had read earlier in a newspaper about Orozco's visit to Asia, but he had never expected to meet him in this country, in this town and in this damn café.

"Is he your...?" he was unable to finish the sentence. She interrupted him.

"Yes," Aurora said. "He is my man, my husband."

"But you are from here...?" he uttered, surprised.

She laughed. He knew that now she was laughing directly at him. She was obviously mocking him, not even trying to hide her spite.

"It shocks you that I slipped through your tight net? You are surprised that I live in Caracas and Beijing, instead of Singapore, Melbourne, Paris or Orange County? You are astonished that my brain did not get conditioned, and that my heart is still beating? And that your people did not manage to drown me in deadly lethargy, as they do almost everyone in this country?"

He felt defenseless. Her tone of voice was harming him. It caused him tremendous pain. Nobody in this country would ever dare to speak to him like this.

Here he was respected. He was a winner, a man fully in control.

Then a thought crossed his mind: 'How much she hates me!'

He heard himself saying defiantly: "Yes. It actually does surprise me. I hardly make mistakes."

He was clearly on the defensive. He was sweating and his hair felt damp, his clothes wet. She was driving him into a corner, with her deadly sarcasm and provocative look, as if he were a filthy roach.

He knew now who she was. He remembered everything suddenly: he recalled her original name, her local name. Aurora was her adopted Spanish *nom de guerre*. She was an artist herself, outrageous and outspoken, dangerous, sharp as a scalpel. She had once been an enemy to be on guard against, a name from the world of art that he was trying to erase from the consciousness of this nation. He had never associated her with Pablo Orozco – he did not know that they were united.

However, what he knew clearly, was that he had fucked up, and that his subordinates had fucked up: 'a tremendous lapse in intelligence,' he thought hysterically. 'An inexcusable blunder on our part.'

She paused. For a split second she awarded

him a look that contained at least some tiny measure of respect. In her own way she acknowledged that for a short moment he did not try to deny anything, which seemed more than she might expect from a man of his kind.

"I worked hard to resist," she said in a matter-of-fact tone. "I worked day and night not to fall into your trap."

They both knew. For a few moments they could converse freely and openly, but only for a few moments.

"Where did the courage come from? The first impulse?"

"Why do you ask? Are you attempting to study my case in order to improve your techniques? So others will not succeed? Are you asking me for information so you can analyze it and become even more effective, so you will be able to block even that tiny crack through which people like me manage to slip through? Are you trying to identify the opening, that error in your otherwise perfect mechanism?"

"Perhaps," he said, impressed and mesmerized by her frankness and foresight. He also took her statement about the 'perfect mechanism' as a compliment. "Most likely, yes."

By now she was in full control. She was tormenting him. But, he realized, he did not want this encounter to end, ever.

He knew he had to regain control. Suddenly, he changed his tactic, tried something totally different. He shrugged his shoulders, waved his hands dismissively and elegantly. He tried to employ at least a bit of charm, the tiny amount that was still left. After all, he was here to represent the great European Culture. Since childhood, he had known how to impress, how to behave, how to act, how to be elegant, convincing and dramatic. At one point in his life, he had even attended acting classes. He knew how to utilize mannerism. Those who sent him here thought about all of this. They had chosen the best man for the job.

He waved his hands, in an old-fashioned, old-world way. Then he smiled and grimaced. Aurora's face did not change.

Suddenly, he felt spent, old and exhausted. He felt like a criminal who had been on the run for too many years, who had finally been caught, arrested and transported to a police station. His mind was torn by confusing contradictory emotions: instinctively he wanted to strangle the guard and escape, or to deny everything. But simultaneously he was possessed by a powerful desire to speak, to confess, and even to volunteer information about all of the offenses and crimes he had been committing for so many years. Actually, he felt relieved. He wanted to be listened to, he wanted to be judged, he wanted to be sentenced, he wanted it, even if such a sequence would lead to severe punishment.

But as a professional, he knew that this was neither the time nor the place to let his guard down and confess everything to her or to anyone else. Especially to her.

Orozco ordered several more dishes for the children, and then addressed a group of local artists. A small crowd had quickly formed around his table. From a distance, he looked like a representative, an ambassador from the new world. Most likely he was simply enjoying himself, trying to bond with his wife's native country. Not much younger than Hans, Orozco looked youthful, almost ageless. Hans knew this was not merely appearance: Orozco was full of ideas. He was active and innovative. He belonged to a very different universe, to an exclusive group of thinkers and artists who stubbornly and decisively refused to abandon art to frivolity and vacuity. Plenty had been written about him: Orozco worked hard, with determination, producing an avalanche of politically and socially charged masterpieces, depicting wars, the terrorist acts of the Empire, the suffering of poor people everywhere, the environmental collapse of the Planet, as well as the great ugliness, even monstrosity, of those torturing the world – the elites, the rulers, the owners of vast wealth. Orozco defended Latin America, Asia, the Middle East and Africa, attacked the Western Empire and its neo-colonialism. He was fearless. In his work, on his canvases, there was hardly any symbolism. Things were depicted concretely and often with shockingly brutal frankness. He always depicted rape as rape, servitude as servitude and plunder as plunder. And he openly identified the white, Western world as the perpetrator, and as the arch tormentor of the Planet. Everyone could easily understand Orozco's art. The messages were right there, screaming and accusing, crystal clear.

"Why do you do this?" she asked, simply, almost gently. "Don't you have any feelings of guilt, at least sometimes ... at least at night?"

"Do what?" But he knew and he knew and he knew. She was too bright, too aware of absolutely everything. She was both his judge and his conscience. From her he could not hide anything.

And with that, he realized he had lost even the tiny bit of respect he had been accorded by her, respect based on a few sparks of honesty. Now he was only buying time – a few seconds, at most, an amount not worth much, but which could, he hoped, allow him to gather his feelings, thoughts and, above all, defenses. He would need to come up with a new plan, in order to survive. He wanted to survive in her eyes, to survive as a man, as a strong, earnest man. He also needed to survive, period, so he could counter-attack and eventually destroy her. This fragile, beautiful woman suddenly became the most important person on earth, or at least in his life: an object of worship, the greatest love and mortal enemy.

"What made you come to this country? What pleasure is there in ruining every tiny spark of hope, every gentle memory about much kinder times, even that little grain of honesty that must still survive somewhere deep within my unfortunate people? There is not much left, don't you see? Why do you want to destroy even that little? Their dignity, their independence, all gone! What more are you trying to take away from them? Everything, absolutely everything?"

He was silent for a while. Then he looked at her – this time he looked straight into her big, deep and beautiful eyes. And as he was looking, his entire body began to shiver. Yes, he wanted her, he adored her, he was in love with her, and at the same time he wanted to destroy her, to rape her brutally, to break all her bones and finally, to throw her mutilated body to the dogs.

"Speak," he said, his voice breaking. "I want to hear your voice. Please say more ... more!"

Was she aware of the storm raging inside him. Did she realize that he was possessed, mad? Perhaps.

She fell silent.

"Speak!" he said, but with a tone of voice, which instead of giving orders, now resembled that of a beggar.

Andre Vltchek

7

Aurora Delivers Her Political Monologues

*E*xcept for the trees, there was nothing attractive about this place. It was so gloomy and dire.

Some trees were vast, consisting of several intertwined trunks and powerful branches of fantastic, fairy-tale shapes. Most formed their own universe, hosting an amazing variety of birds, insects and tropical flowers. The trees were proud and incorruptible. They stood tall, when not cut brutally down. This evening they reached into the night sky through a gauze of clouds.

Aurora's eyes caressed the trees she had known and admired since her early childhood.

These complex and ancient beings (she had always believed in their souls) were what she desperately missed, living on the other side of the world. She remembered and talked to them from a great distance. She painted them, again and again, from memory and from old photos she always carried.

"They are cutting down my trees," she whispered, almost forgetting she was not alone. "They are cutting them down all over this archipelago. They murder trees for profit. There is almost nothing left to love here, except for blurry, abstract memories. And some of those memories belong to a distant past, even to the period long before I was born."

"Pardon me?" Hans did not understand. Or he pretended not to.

She was not talking to him, of that much he was aware. She was talking to herself, and to the trees.

"Nothing." Her mind quickly returned to this cursed café, and she lowered her eyes to the ground from the magnificent, divine and wide treetops spreading above her head. She was in front of the face she despised. The face confronted her with a sickening mixture of angst, hatred and lust. Clearly a dishonest, treacherous and crooked face. She wanted to remain in the trees. She wanted to caress and greet every branch and every leaf but knew she was needed down here, on this filthy and debased Earth, in the middle of this intellectual sewer.

She held her silence. Deep inside she made

a personal pledge: one day she would return to paint, to immortalize these ancient trees, before all were cut down, before everything here finally stopped and died, consumed, irreversibly, by ravenous greed and selfishness and fatal indifference. "When I return, I will paint you directly, not from old photographs. I will spend weeks here, working. And then, I will bring images of you with me, beloved trees. We will go to many parts of the world together. I will explain to everyone, on all continents, how beautiful you are. In this way, you will never die. In this way, they will never manage to murder you."

Then she spoke to Hans:

"Using your network of snitches and agents, you sniff around this miserable country, my broken land. You identify those people who are still capable of breathing freely, who are resisting - those who can think and who have at least some dignity and principles left. You search for those who are not yet fully sold and corrupt. You want to find them in order to destroy them. You don't kill them physically as your Empire did in the not so distant past. Instead you buy them, you debase them, you castrate them, you tie their tubes. If they refuse to obey you, then you make them irrelevant, you erase their names from public consciousness, and in this way you gag them forever. You or your kind do the same in Africa, in the Middle East, in Oceania and in all other parts of Asia. We managed to stop you in Latin America, in China and Russia, but almost

everywhere else you rampage. You are not
creative even in how you destroy people. You
use old tactics invented and perfected centuries
ago by the colonialists. Immediately after you
scare your victims out of their wits, or after you
fully corrupt them, or both, you convert them
into your slaves. You order what to say or write
or paint. You instruct them how to lie. You do it
so that your white race and the Western fascist
regime can retain power. Your exploitation of
the arts makes the exploitation of the economy,
the land and the culture easier and complete.
You rule, but you are empty and there is no
optimism inside you, no creative zeal, and no
humanity. You don't want humanity to
advance. You don't even know what decency is.
You overflow with nihilism, with dark sarcasm,
and your regime is totally lethal. It perverts all
that is good and pure in human beings, it ruins
all that is worth living and fighting for."

*Mozart: As a Communist and
internationalist, you knew all this when you
were still alive, Bertolt! I envy you. In my
days, we were so blind. We did not think about
such things.*

*Brecht: But now, in Germany and
elsewhere, they are trying to re-write history.
Even about me... The lies they are spreading...
But yes, of course, I was aware of all that she
is saying. And in my own way, I fought
against their fascist system, day and night. As
both of us, you and I, fight against it now.*

Aurora continued speaking in her even tone. Hans continued listening without interrupting, facing her, mesmerized still, full of longing and lust and fear, perspiring, hoping he might confuse her, overpower her, and win.

"You hate everything related to Latin America, to Iran, to Russia, and of course to China, because you cannot accept that some country or a continent could be proud and big and strong but peaceful, that it could be based on a culture that is much older and greater than your own, that it is Communist or socialist on its own terms, that it does all it can to improve the lives of millions of ordinary people. You search for every piece of dirt related to such countries, you feed their every little error into your propaganda machine. You inflate miniscule mistakes and belittle grandiose achievements. You can't stand it when some Asian nation succeeds, especially when a Communist Asian nation does. In recent history, your people have murdered millions, tens of millions, of innocent people on this continent: in Korea and Vietnam, Cambodia and Laos, and of course here! So-called human rights are only for your white race: everywhere else you murder people left and right, because they are not really human, so why should human rights apply to sub-humans? Your propaganda is racist and fanatical, and as one-sided as that of your allies, of ISIS and the Pentecostals, but perhaps even more so, because your empire actually manufactured both ISIS and the Christian fundamentalists. You are spreading lies, and as a result of your indoctrination, black becomes white and white becomes black. War becomes peace and rape is confused with love. The most oppressive regimes like those that reign here or in Thailand, the Philippines or India are promoted as 'democracies' and called 'tolerant.' You actually manufacture those regimes, and then you sustain them and disseminate their deadly seeds all over the world.

You managed to convince your own people, and even many of our people, that being white makes you correct, that your race and culture are exceptional and superior, unique and well above all other races and cultures in the world!

All your arguments would collapse in any free and open debate, but there is no debate because the BBC, FOX, CNN, DW and dozens of other fully funded propaganda outlets are always at your disposal, would never allow people like me or my husband to confront all the prefabricated dogmas and lies. As institutions of corporate empire, they never question your supremacy, their supremacy, and the supremacy of global dictatorship: ideological, political and economic.

Every place, every nation where people enthusiastically work for the benefit of their own nation, is labeled a 'dictatorship.'

You work to systematically destroy the nations where enormous public parks, sidewalks, theaters, public transportation, hospitals and sport centers are built for the people. You support countries where there are no public spaces left, where water is privatized, where poor people simply die if they get sick and where children get terrible educations in overcrowded classes or in schools oriented to business or religion. Yes, you love private schools and the cities choked on exhaust fumes from stinking cars and scooters. You actually love slums and misery, and segregated societies with mass-produced shopping malls and chain hotels, constructed next to open gutters. You love pop culture, because the more brainless our people become, the easier it is to control and to fool them!"

Hans could not utter a single word. Aurora spoke and he listened, that was all. But he observed with great attention. He saw and registered each tiny wrinkle around her eyes, the color of her skin and hair, the way she threw words at him.

Mozart: That is correct: they implement the lowest pop culture. They do it all over the world. They keep bragging about people like me, and about our brother Beethoven, Comrade Chopin and Commander Shostakovich. But what they actually put upon poor and desperate people are not our symphonies, operas and etudes, but violent action and horror films and brainless soap operas.

Brecht: They also destroyed all traditional, popular and deep forms of theater on that miserable archipelago. Every form of art that was interactive, where people could participate, was smashed. What followed was total silence, emptiness. And the void was gradually filled with television sets, the silence replaced with an outrageous loud stupidity of modified and even more dumbed-down Western pop.

Mozart: So true! But how do you know all that?

Brecht: I travelled there for two months with Maxim Gorky. We were appalled.

"You convert artists into decorators, thinkers into primitive, vulgar entertainers. You know how to celebrate this prostitution, this treason, in style, by throwing lavish cocktail parties for your intellectual hookers who are flown to Berlin and London and Amsterdam, where you make them speak, shamelessly, about the enormity of their destroyed culture..."

He swallowed hard. He cleared his throat. He lifted his eyes, and then he looked directly at her, again, counterattacking:

"Well, it really is enormous, isn't it?" He searched for signs of support around him, but his disciples who were not currently engaged with Orozco were now all silent, some even looking down. Dozens of eyes drilled him, or at least he imagined so. "The culture, this culture, your culture ... it is enormous, don't you think so?"

For the first time, Aurora lost her temper. She replied loudly, angrily:

"It used to be, before it was totally smashed.

Before your governments decided that they could not tolerate our nationalists, before they could not accept that we had one of the largest Communist parties on earth, which happened to behave democratically ... before you planned and sponsored a horrific coup, not unlike those coups you sponsored in Latin America, but here it was much more sinister, much bloodier and deadlier ... before you helped to form this fascist dictatorship and then supplied it with all the necessary know-how, assisting it in incarcerating and killing everybody capable of thinking, including our intellectuals and half our teachers. Our traditional forms of theatre were crushed, our film studios closed down, our beautiful classical music silenced, and books burned! The rivers were clogged with corpses ... millions executed, mass graves ... unimaginable torture and land-grabs, sweeping privatization ... total destruction of logic, arts. Poetry died, and soon after compassion. You turned this poor nation into a mental asylum, a horrific noisy den, a filthy stale swamp. Yes, before all that, we had our own, our great culture!"

"It is a thriving democracy now," he said. "People can vote again."

"Vote? Vote for whom? You made our people thoroughly ignorant. They know more about religion – your old and lethal ally – than about logic or ethics. They have no ideology. People vote for oligarchs or the clowns backed by pro-business thugs. Political parties throw pop concerts and spread cash and crumbs of food during their election campaigns. It's almost like in India, or perhaps worse. Or people vote for cruel military officers, disguised as politicians. They vote for the same people who have been stealing from them, day and night, for decades. They vote for the former generals – war criminals, some of them. Some of those Generals married daughters of much older Generals who were responsible for millions of people murdered or disappeared during and after the coup, or in the occupied territories! They are voting for political parties that left nothing public in this country, for the parties that made sure the parks were surrounded by barbed wire and converted into golf courses for the elites. They vote for political parties that made sure poor people couldn't even cross the street since there are almost no crossings left. They have to drive to the next roundabout and then return from the other side, if they have money to purchase fuel and their own vehicle."

"It is the people's choice to vote these parties in."

"Their choice? It is never their choice. All Marxist parties are banned – those that could truly represent the interests of the people. All socialist theories are banned and for years even words like "class" were forbidden. People are taught only about consumerism and capitalism. They are educated by advertisement. They are conditioned to admire what ruins them and robs them. First you slaughter their bodies, then you slaughter their minds. Unless people are truly free and educated, unless they realize into what misery they have been thrown, there is no choice! How can they vote freely if they are constantly intimidated and blinded from seeing how horribly they are being robbed?"

Aurora couldn't stop. Now she was shouting at Hans, and at all those people who stared at her with unconcealed surprise, even shock.

"And who says that Asia must follow the Western multi-party system? Democracy translates from Greek as "rule of the people," not as "multi-party regime." Who says that we must ape our colonizers? Is the multi-party system working so very well in the West? Definitely not, and you know it better than I do! The system is there only to guarantee inertia, and the status quo. Why should we, with our cultures that are much older than those of Europe, be forced to follow a corrupt scheme? Our societies formerly functioned on a totally different platform and they were much more peaceful and more just, before Western powers arrived and began terrorizing, stripping and colonizing the entire world."

She was now breathing heavily:

"What propels you Hans G? How did it all begin? Once you were a boy. You also had dreams. Your mother read you fairytales. How did it happen that you became a thug?"

Several people formed a circle around them. Some even put down their mobile phones, something almost unimaginable in this part of the world, where mobile phones were used in every cinema, during all family outings, and, it was said, even during sex. Hans was aware that they were being observed, but he was not much concerned about the local artists. He knew them all too well. Behind the facade, he despised them profoundly. He despised their flimsy attempts at manufacturing hot emotions to sell for cold cash. They were all whores. He knew the local artists had virtually no principles and almost no understanding of the world. Very few of them had even any talent. They could not understand much that was being discussed tonight – their English was too basic and their knowledge of the subject limited. This exchange touched them directly, but it was clear that many registered only sounds, accents, intonations and were not capable of grasping true meaning. Perhaps Aurora thought they would be shocked by her words. But Hans knew very well: they were shocked only by the tone of her voice, by her shouting at him.

Aurora was right. Hans was fully aware of the fact that in the 60 years after the West-sponsored killing fields, one of the most impressive achievements of the imposed regime was its ability to force people into total intellectual lethargy and imbecility. Almost nobody here appeared to think logically. Those who still could, were in their eighties, educated and formed long before the coup. After the bloodletting, thinking and serious discussions were fully discouraged. The regime managed to produce several new generations of young men and women perfectly oblivious of, detached from and disinterested in the dreadful reality of their society. The methodology of how to brainwash the nation was imported and then calibrated to fit local conditions. He knew all this was to his favor, not to hers. 'You will never get through to them!' he addressed Aurora in his mind: 'You never will. They are my servants, my slaves. They are not much, but they are mine.'

But what he thought and what he said publicly was always different.

"Bunk conspiracy theory," uttered Hans G, once again trying to sound nonchalant and light. He tried one of his tricks again: he smiled at Aurora, patronizingly.

"Oh, a conspiracy theory? Look around: there are only your lackeys in this place."

"You're so patronizing," said Hans.

Political correctness was his trump card – it always worked. It was a great anti-toxin for accusations such as hers – a remedy perfected for decades by Western mass media and academia. Thank god, by now everything was well worked out and under control – the system did not leave anything to chance. Ideologues from top universities and research centers were ready to provide advice and guidance, developing and delivering linguistic somersaults, pirouettes, dogmas. Yes, the name of the anti-toxin administered to confront revolution was 'political correctness.' And it was put to work whenever all arguments were exhausted. If a country was ruined, swimming in shit, it would be impolite, 'politically incorrect.' to say so, because it could "touch sensitivities" of the "local people" – namely 'elites.' If nobody was capable of thinking anymore, the result of several decades of systematic brainwashing and indoctrination concealed as 'education' – most of it sponsored and administered by Western media, institutions, scholarships and grants – then political correctness could not be contested. It threatened anyone who dared to define and describe what was clearly in front of their eyes. Racists and supremacists, foreign and local, those who broke the spines of entire nations and continents, could effortlessly turn things around and accuse their critics of racism and intolerance.

Mozart: "Do you think Aurora could be silenced?"
Brecht: "Unlikely."

"Patronizing?" she replied. "Let's talk to at least one recipient of your grants." She turned to her left, to face a man in his early 50s, who was now wearing, like almost all the other men there, a black T-shirt, a shapeless pair of jeans, and worn rubber sandals. Along with the others, he was smoking clove cigarettes. "This person, for instance: I believe he once enjoyed a reputation of being a 'true revolutionary filmmaker'?"

She spoke to him in her native tongue:
"My husband and I would be interested in producing a short film – a document about my

return home, this short visit. I have in mind a film that would let me speak about injustice in this land and about how dramatically this place differs, in spirit, from the revolutionary countries where I now live and work: Venezuela, Ecuador, Brazil, Bolivia and China. We don't have a budget, yet – we are putting our own time and resources into the project. But we think that such a film would make a big difference here. Would you be interested in working with us even if no money is involved? Would you be interested in editing the footage for the cause?"

A sly grin appeared on the filmmaker's face. He did not say anything. He kept puffing on his clove cigarette, giving Aurora an openly cynical and even insulting look.

She knew that in this country, by saying that she had no money to disperse, she was stating that she had no power, that she was an absolute failure, in fact a contemptible being. Money was all that mattered.

She paused, taking in the entire scene.

Then she mimicked his crooked smirk:

"And there is one more project – a business one, high-profile." She drilled him with her eyes: "It pays regular editing fees, those offered by the industry. We could pay around 2,000 US dollars for a quick job. The film would be short. It would be used as an advertisement for dog food."

She paused.

"Are you interested?"

"Of course!" came the immediate reply. His

grin dissolved. The filmmaker suddenly appeared eager and deeply respectful. He even stopped puffing smoke from his clove cigarette directly into Aurora's face.

Sharply, she turned back to Hans: "I rest my case!"

"Disgusting. Patronizing," said Hans. "The way you talk to him, the way you fool him: it makes me unwell. How could you treat a human being like this?"

"This used to be my country," she said, slowly, ignoring his hypocritical lament. " But you are now in control here. Even this man is your creation, your tiny monster, a Frankenstein. There is almost nothing that I recognize here, anymore."

An old waiter was now serving nauseating over-sweetened tea and substantial plates of fried rice. Everyone got his or her dish and a cup, a tiny courtesy of the cultural center. Otherwise no one would come.

"Your country? You even changed your name, and you became Aurora."

"Because there is nothing here that is mine, anymore. Even my own language has been changed, into some revolting fusion. My culture has been murdered. Your ideologues forced everyone to listen to fifty year old American songs, with little variation. People listen to them, and then they sing them at karaoke bars, in cafes, even in clubs. They are lobotomized, they move like lunatics. That's your cultural diversity, Hans G! Thank you! Here, people are dying from hunger, they shit into canals from which they later take water, they are decimated by a lack of decent medical care, but they shout that they are actually not poor, that they are doing well. They believe that they live in a democracy, even as their village chiefs and husbands and fathers order them how to vote. You helped to convert this nation into a crowd of brain-dead idiots! You created a nation that can't write one decent book, stage one decent play, build an airplane, nor even pave a sidewalk or dig an underpass or a gutter! You created the nation that lives only from plundering its own natural resources on behalf of foreign companies. Do you know what will happen when there are no more trees to cut down and no more minerals and oil to extract? People here will starve! They will eat their own crap, or they will eat each other! It will happen soon. But the elites will immediately leave, to places where they can enjoy their loot. They all have houses and condominiums in Singapore, Australia, California and Hong Kong! They all have one-way business class tickets out of this country.

"I am only here to introduce Beethoven to the people of this land," said Hans, charmingly. A sophisticated, saintly smile once again appeared on his face. "Periodically I invite choirs."

Mozart: [roaring laughter]
Brecht: [roaring laughter]
Mozart: Let's get some more wine before I continue.

"And you do many other things, don't you? You stage photo exhibitions depicting the brutality of the Polish Communist government during the 1980s! And nobody even pukes. You do it in this country, where between 2 and 3 million perished, slaughtered in the name of the war against Communism. Where the Communist Party is still banned. How many people died in Gdansk, in Poland. Two? Five? How many people died during the Soviet intervention in Czechoslovakia? One hundred? Probably less. 3 million died here, while further millions were slaughtered all over Indochina ... Why not show that?"

He let her talk. He was not troubled by this – such arguments represented no threat to him. Numbers, especially when they went to millions, were too abstract for local people. At the end it really did not matter whether 2 or 5 or 7 million Vietnamese, Laotian or Cambodian civilians died during the American War. It did not matter whether 6 or 10 million continued to die in the Democratic Republic of Congo. Those millions in the Middle East did not matter. He was well aware of the fact that with a few dozen good ideologists and academics, an example of those few people who perished in Poland or Czechoslovakia could be used to counter-balance the tens or hundreds of millions of people who were murdered by the West in Africa, Asia and Latin America.

"I am just a head of a cultural center."

"You are an agent, Hans G. A snitch... A

corruptor..."

"Prove it!" And then in a whisper: "And even if I am, what can you do?"

Once again he felt confident, at least for the moment. He was now on familiar turf. She was obviously still shocked by numbers. 'Good,' he thought 'Let her play with numbers. It's a futile game.' He was not afraid of numbers, especially when the numbers were enormous, surging into millions. A man could not really imagine a million crushed balls, only his own.

Andre Vltchek

PART – II

Götterdämmerung

Andre Vltchek

8

Aurora's Murdered Sister Remembered

*T*he next blow came from a totally unexpected direction.

"My sister," Aurora said. Just these two words, like two bullets aimed at his chest.

He exhaled loudly.

"What about her?"

Hans didn't really know whom she was talking about, but a strange intuition assaulted him without mercy, an extremely bad intuition, potentially a fatal one. His discomfort was nauseating. His bladder screamed. His bowels threatened to explode.

"You knew her."

"What are you talking about?"

Aurora spoke her name. He knew her. He had collected information about her activities, before finally passing everything on to his colleagues. He had met her twice, face to face, though he had not been in charge of the case. What's more, although he had been very close to that ill-fated event, in the end it was not he who made the final decision.

"I heard about what happened," he whispered. "I am very sorry. I didn't know she was your sister."

Suddenly more words flew out of him:

"Aurora, listen, I swear it wasn't me. I really didn't..."

She looked away. Then her eyes stopped at the trunk of an ancient tree. She embraced it, with her mind, her soul.

"That much I know," she said.

Smoke from the clove cigarettes now bothered his throat and eyes. The feeling of discomfort intensified. Right now he wanted to be far away from here, in a remote and serene place: perhaps in Northern Hokkaido or Central Vietnam but anywhere really, as long as it were really far, very far away from here.

"One day after they found her body in the middle of the road ... at night ... at least four influential European daily newspapers decided to run the story about how tolerant was the local political system, the culture ... how moderate are the local religions."

"Just coincidence," he said.

"No," she said. "My sister fought both: your fundamentalist religious implants, and the Western political and economic control over this part of the world. She knew that everything was inter-connected. She knew that the Protestants destroyed this country; their imported preachers worked very hard to trigger the bloodbath – before, during and after the coup. And she knew that Islam was derailed by them, and forced into what it is now. She could name names. And she was extremely vocal. She published several reports on the topic."

He did not reply. He felt nauseated. He felt old. He was not up to this fight. She was too powerful and she knew too much. He was petrified that she would begin dropping names ... right here, in front of everybody.

"I am sorry," he said finally. "I don't know what else to say."

Andre Vltchek

9

Dragons And Boozing Painters in Berlin

*A*urora searched for answers and consolation far above the surface of the Earth, in the clouds that embraced her dragons. The wide branches of ancient trees and dragons were closely related. As the moon shone through the clouds, she swore she could identify distinct contours of at least two mighty creatures, their eyes shining and angry staring at the people below. She believed in dragons – not in the evil ones invented by twisted European storytellers to scare little children. She believed in mighty and sacred dragons, in the enormous, wise and kind Asian beings with long whiskers and sad deep eyes that had for millennia inhabited China, Vietnam, Korea and Japan. There were many fantastic dragons in all corners of Asia: from the flying ones in the north, to the water dragons living at the bottom of the murky waters of Mekong River where they were called *Nagas*. All over Asia, dragons were worshipped, profoundly respected and sincerely loved. Aurora had taught her husband how to comprehend and admire her dragons. She read him countless stories, showed him old Chinese and Japanese drawings, until, at some point, he began painting them with devotion and passion. On his canvases they waged wars against oppression, they fought epic battles confronting foreign invaders. They were always on the side of powerless peasants and voiceless victims. In some of his work they gently taught children in poor parts of the world about life, nature, kindness, compassion, justice and pride.

"One day, a sacred mountain will open," Aurora often whispered to her husband at night. "Tens of mighty dragons, maybe hundreds, maybe thousands, maybe tens of thousands, will fly toward the corners of the world where human beings are tormented and humiliated. With them, justice will finally arrive."

"Maybe that's why they hate dragons in the West," smiled Orozco. "There they suspect that with the dragons will arrive the end of Western reign over our poor Planet."

He was now advancing that moment. Inspired by the stories told by his wife, he invited those tremendous mighty creatures to join the vanguard of the revolution. And on his canvases they did.

Brecht: And they are about to join, in real life. We are trying to work out with them some minor strategic details.

Mozart: I've heard that once they are fully awake, they must eat, and that some are as big as aircraft carriers, and they can fly like rockets.

Brecht: They fly so fast...

Mozart: That's a lot of calories, a lot of fuel... When they are in full combat mode, they have to be, so to speak, refueled.

Brecht: In short they have to be fed... Like us... Except that they are millions of times bigger than us... But we will figure out how, soon...

*

Aurora smiled at the dragons. They looked after her, she thought. They protected her. Whenever she spotted dragons, whenever she sensed their presence, she knew she was back in Asia. No matter how devastated the country, this was still her world. The dragons were her companions, her protectors, her big, loyal brothers and sisters.

Hans G had his own allies, but they all lived on the surface of the Earth. Now two local artists approached him, both just returned from a two-week trip to Berlin, where their paintings had been displayed in two rather prestigious galleries. Hans had made sure that in Europe they were welcomed with open arms. Leading critics had been invited. Television crews filmed the opening. The exhibition was a roaring success. The topic of their artwork was called "Comparing Movements of Hands and Feet in Various Southeast Asian Traditional Dances." Before exhibiting their canvases in Europe, they had spent months researching, painting, drinking and copulating with the local women on two remote islands of the archipelago, all expenses covered by the Cultural Institute.

This was their 'new period,' a sharp departure from the past, from deeply engaged political art. Both had formerly painted the horrors of poverty, the exhausted bodies of farmers after inhuman labor in fields owned by corrupt local feudal lords. They had formerly painted village women with empty and desperate gazes, with wrinkled faces and broken bodies. They had formerly painted children – abused and suffering from malnutrition. They had formerly painted the beggars and slums surrounding enormous shopping malls in the cities. Several years ago, little by little their work had begun to enter the subconsciousness of the nation. Naturally, something had to be done. The messages painted by their brushes were too strong, challenging the dogmas of market fundamentalism and local feudalism. Orders came from above. Hans G was told to 'take care' of this unfortunate situation. And he did take care of it, with his usual determination, elegance and discretion. Both painters were invited to his office, offered strong coffee and tasty cakes, treated with great, even exaggerated respect. Hans told them that they had been selected to represent their country abroad. They were presented with a detailed plan, and showed impressive photographs of the gallery that was ready to invite them, sponsor their trip and exhibit their work. They were given fliers of a lovely historic hotel in the center of Berlin where they were expected to spend two full weeks, of course all expenses paid. It was explained that they would be rewarded with generous daily allowances and two sets of Lufthansa tickets. All in exchange for very little, or almost nothing: instead of canvases depicting misery and horrors, they would carry with them some twenty paintings depicting traditional dances. Ten paintings produced by each artist. They were expected to concentrate on the elegance and sensuality of the movements produced by the hands, feet and eyes of the performers.

Both artists were shocked. They had nothing to do with traditional dances. They tried to negotiate the substance of their exhibition. Surely the European audience would be interested in seeing how the majority of the people of this archipelago suffered every day. "No," insisted Hans. "That period is over! You can visit hundreds of art galleries in Paris or Berlin, and see for yourself – there is absolutely no political art on display there. Suffering and deprivation is for the UNDP, not for the world of art. This is the era of experimental forms and of beauty."

A heated debate lasted exactly forty-five minutes. During that time, the per diem was increased, an expensive *Bordeaux* was served, and the deal was sealed.

*

Both painters were immensely impressed by the German capital. They were given a celebrity welcome. They felt appreciated and for that they were endlessly grateful to Hans and his contacts. They forgot all about their countrymen and women, about neo-colonialism, feudalism, corruption and the misery back home. Their German hosts, critics and journalists artfully tickled their egos, repeating from morning to night that such exceptional artists 'were the best ambassadors of their culture – true builders of bridges between various great civilizations.'

Formed by a culture which, except for a brief two decades, had always served humiliating colonial masters, they were used to feeling profound inferiority when dealing with the ruling Western race. But in Berlin, tall blond men and women prepared their meals, served them in restaurants, washed their clothes, and sang loud odes to their work. It took their breath away.

This was their first journey abroad. They wanted to try everything. On the second day in Berlin, before the media marathon began, they went out drinking and wound up in a modestly priced whorehouse. Out of timidity, they opted for two women from Cebu City. The next day they became much more daring. They hit several local pubs, downing dozens of tall half-liter glasses of beer mixed with jam, Berlin's specialty. They drank and drank, until almost two in the morning, and then puked all over the perfectly laid cobblestone of Museum Island, almost falling under the wheels of a slow moving police patrol car. The cops checked their passports and then displayed great delight at how well these two Muslim lads had adapted to the European culture! "Hey Fritz, they drink and puke just like us!" one of the cops declared, impressed, patting the artists on their shoulders.

On the way back to their hotel, the two artists picked up a young and stoned single mother from Leipzig who had come to the capital to visit her aunt. They convinced her to come with them, shared her on a single bed in one of their rooms, and drank some more, puked loudly again, this time all three of them, from the window, and finally, the next day, they managed to visit several well-known museums of the city, including the *Pergamon*.

In the following days they were interviewed on several occasions. The local press was extremely kind – several newspapers wrote short reviews and a radio station interviewed them about the cultural diversity and the beauty of their country.

Now they came to thank Hans for his support and patronage.

"We will do it again," said Hans, smiling.

"We will do it very soon, maybe in Rome or Paris."

The three of them embraced, a heartfelt fraternal hug, big smiles and patting. A true international *Bruderschaft*! A total hoax, but the artists could not care less, too carried away by the game, too intoxicated with their own success and suddenly bright future. The poor masses of this archipelago had suddenly moved elsewhere, far away, as if a distant nightmare had dissolved into the bright, cheerful colors of an optimistic dawn.

When the painters left, Hans turned to Aurora who was now seated at the corner of a long table, periodically lifting her eyes, communicating with her dragons and trees, too embarrassed to concentrate fully on what was happening around her, down on Earth.

"I know you don't want to hear it, but the purpose of my being in this country is nothing other than to promote arts, culture, as well as building cultural bridges between our wonderful people."

She felt tired. She felt embarrassed looking at him, at this aging man, with his disgraceful game, his lies.

"How can you sleep at night?" she said.

He ignored her words.

"No matter what you think about me personally, one thing can't be denied: the local artists and thinkers can draw inspiration from European inquisitiveness and courage."

"Courage?" she wondered. "Socrates," she said. "But that was a long time ago. Giordano

Bruno, but he was convicted of heresy by the Church, and burned at the stake over four centuries ago, hanged upside-down and gagged, naked. Jose Saramago and Harold Pinter, but they have passed on, although only recently. And these are not the ones you are promoting here, Hans G."

Andre Vltchek

10

Hans G Daydreams About Raping Aurora

*N*ow it was Orozco's turn, to drive nails into the "Culture". He slowly turned around making eye contact with several local artists. His sarcastic glance pierced them, a mocking smile plied his lips:

"One week ago, on the way here, we made a brief stop in Paris, and I went to the Louvre..."

'What now? What is *he* going to say about *the Culture*?' Hans felt his entire body overwhelmed by a powerful spasm. He experienced a sharp, physical pain. But perhaps he only imagined it; maybe his discomfort was psychological, rising from the bottom of his soul.

Orozco now stood right behind him, almost

touching his back, the huge bearish Orozco with that deep sardonic voice. The man making gentle origami for the poor local children had suddenly vanished. Without warning he had been replaced by an extremely dangerous revolutionary artist – the famous, combative and uncompromising South American warrior.

Unexpectedly Hans felt the hand of Orozco squeezing his shoulder. The hand was impressively heavy, powerful but at the same time soft. Hans thought: 'This hand, this huge hand of a strong and fearless man caresses her breasts at night, searches for the moisture between her legs, savors it, enjoys her entire body. This hand touches her face, covers her naked body with a comforter, and dries her tears when she cries. This hand feeds her when she is ill and supports her when she feels weak. It catches her when she stumbles, prevents her from falling. But why?' Hans knew. Hans knew that Aurora was fearless, intelligent, committed, beautiful, principled, and ... alive.

Then, for a short moment, Hans submerged into the swamp of his deep-rooted Germanic romanticism. He thought: 'I would give anything on earth for the privilege of being loved by this woman.' That was what he thought. That was what he made himself think. Frankly, it was just an experiment. At least once more he wanted to experience thinking and feeling this way. And it actually felt good. It brought him back, some thirty years, to those days when he was still willing to sacrifice almost anything and everything – wealth, career, even power – for just one night or even one single passionate embrace with a celestial being, a woman of his dreams.

For a moment he disconnected himself from Orozco's hand and voice and he tried to imagine himself and Aurora together, in his bedroom, late at night. 'Now she is mine' he thought – he repeated it to himself, he tried to imagine it. He also tried to recall the tenderness he once used to feel toward other people, especially toward women who had entered his life and whom he cared for. But to his horror, no tenderness was left; it had evaporated. What remained was a potent physical almost animalistic urge. He knew instinctively that Orozco had never lost his tenderness, even at his age. He knew it was not just brute physical and mental strength that this enormous man offered the world. He feared and hated Orozco for his warmth, for his humanity. He was envious, jealous of him, and he did not know how to imitate him, nor how to destroy him in that moment.

Then Hans let his imagination go unchecked, into its by now typical course. Step by step he recalled the most brutal acts to which he had subjected so many women of this country, women that he had first bought and then mercilessly violated. He wanted to do something even more evil to Aurora, something more painful and humiliating. He imagined her hands tied, and he grabbed her slender shoulders, pulled her by her hair, dragged her screaming across the floor, threw her onto his vast bed, squeezed her neck, pushed her face deep into a pillow, then plastered her with his weight and finally, forcefully sodomized her, right under the scorn-filled eyes of his beloved European composer -- Wolfgang Amadeus Mozart.

He could hear her scream. He could feel her pain. He could imagine his own delight and savoring of the victory.

His summer chinos made of expensive light cotton were now stretched in the front. Hans G was having a mighty public erection, clearly visible, garishly illuminated by the dim light of the cafe.

'At least I can rape you in my dreams,' he thought. 'This is what I really want. I could not care less about your feelings, or my own, about tenderness. I want to show you where you really belong! In my dreams, I will disappear your man, then cut off his balls and push them down his throat, at some provincial police station. And then I will drag you into an abandoned barn. There I will tie you up and enjoy your body, repeatedly, for many days and nights. Afterwards, to feel fully satisfied, I will finish you off with the single and powerful blow of a metal bar. You see, that is the true Culture of mine! That is the hidden but true essence of my damned continent! We have been doing this to cunts like you everywhere, for all these long centuries and millennia.'

He was breathing heavily. In a single night he had experienced dozens of contradictory emotions: pride and superiority, humiliation and fear, total despair, and now, an overwhelming desire to plunder, violate and kill.

He was sweating, because he was also feeling defeated. But his penis was hard because he still harbored hope for a final victory. To Hans, victory was synonymous with possession, control, and plunder.

Brecht: I suspect he had done such things many times before?

Mozart: Raping? Yes, though not many times. Hans considered himself to be something of a gentleman, ideally. A gentleman, in his conception, raped only upon occasion. What's more – Hans never murdered his victims personally. He always employed his subordinates to do the job.

Andre Vltchek

11

Orozco Drives Nails Into the Gloomy Coffin Of Western Culture

Orozco, as if feeling the obsessive and obscene wave of emotions emanate from Hans, stopped talking abruptly and withdrew his hand. Then he noticed the prominent swelling at the front part of Hans G's trousers. 'Triggered by my brief, friendly gesture?' he wondered

"You went to the Louvre, *mi amor*," Aurora reminded her husband, trying to disrupt the short awkward silence.

She also noticed that obnoxious growth deforming the otherwise elegant pants of the man she had confronted a few moments earlier.

Hans could not control himself now even if

he had wanted to. Foul images filled him, extremely violent images, explicit and pornographic. He did not try to suppress them. 'Orozco mentioned the *Musee du Louvre*,' he thought. 'There are plenty of graphic depictions of kidnappings, torture and rape ... in all sections and floors. Rape is one of the essential forms of art. *Es ist auch ein Kunst!*'

He realized that he wanted to do to Aurora exactly what others had done to her sister. He knew exactly what had been done to her. His subordinates had told him everything in detail. For months he had fantasized about what he had heard. He had not been the one who had performed those acts, which he had regretted profusely.

'Carl Jung. Jung thought that the entire European culture was sick, pathological ... that it was a culture of plunderers and mass murderers. Was he correct? Yes, he was. And so what? I cannot deny my essence, my nature,' thought Hans. 'I want this country at my feet, and I want this woman on her stomach, screaming. I cannot accept merely being treated like a criminal by her. I want to actually be one. I want to be a real criminal, a monster, the most shameless sort!'

*

"I slowly walked from *Jeu de Paume* on *Place de la Concorde* towards the Louvre," said Orozco. "It was cold and misty outside. Parisians drifted through the *Jardin des*

Tuileries near the ancient bookstalls on the banks of the Seine. They looked sad and lost like ships passing each other in a fog. Their raincoats like sails, hats and scarves like symbols and flags of surrender. You would not believe it, but the upper part of the Eiffel Tower was hidden in the clouds or in a thick fog, as if it were disappearing into nothingness. It was all stunningly beautiful and at the same time endlessly sad! That day, melancholy was everywhere, even inside my own soul. Perhaps it was not such a good day to visit the grand old godfather of all French cultural institutions.

By then I thought that I was fairly familiar with the Louvre, entering those sacred halls and chambers so many times, on hundreds of occasions, since I was a young man. I studied in Paris for five years. But this time I saw my visit simply as a courtesy call, almost like ... paying respects to my good old and very sick friend."

"Why sick?" asked one local poet, surprised.

Orozco paused, looked at a young man, and then replied, slowly: "I don't really know. I felt it. Maybe because its importance had vanished ... its luster had worn off ... maybe because he or she or it – whatever the Louvre really is, as I don't deny that it may be, after all, a living organism – seemed too worn-out, with no desire left to say anything significant. These days, only a few artists go there to learn about art and to dream..."

"I remember that day, as I refused to enter," said Aurora. "The museum felt so intimidating and cold. But I let you go. I waited for you in one of the museum cafés, underground, reading '*Seeing*' by Saramago," recalled Aurora. She was speaking to her husband and to him alone.

"Yes, *mi amor*. You did not want to go." He addressed his wife with the formal *Usted*. Then he switched back to English. "I had no desire to see anything in particular, either. That day I did not come to visit the great masters like Delacroix, or Goya."

"You like Delacroix?" hissed Hans, sarcastically.

"Of course," replied the Venezuelan revolutionary artist. "Almost as much as I love Murillo and Goya and El Greco and Liang Kai and Tang Yin and Josetsu."

The local students looked baffled. They knew absolutely nothing about Asian art, except the few contemporary anti-Communist painters – darlings of the Western establishment and anti-Chinese propaganda – like Ai Weiwei. And the only reason they had heard about them was because they were also supported and promoted by the Western cultural centers.

"I stood in line in front of the Louvre for almost an hour. Again, thousands of visitors from all over the world were queuing, talking, taking photos of each other and themselves on their mobile phones. I listened to people's chatting; almost none of them had any interest in art. Almost nobody discussed anything related to the Museum. They came here merely because, while in Paris, they felt obliged to visit the Louvre. There were Europeans, North Americans, Asians, Latin Americans and Africans. The Louvre had become a brand. Several decades ago, Western art had become fashion. Matisse and Prada, Renoir and Louis Vuitton. Armed guards with machine guns patrolled outside. Obnoxious security agents checked visitors inside the Pyramid entry. I paid the admission fee and passed through a metal detector, then walked through one of the entrances. I took an escalator. My movements were almost mechanical, like those of a sleepwalker. I had no particular plan. I had no idea what I was searching for. I walked and walked through those magnificent rooms decorated with enormous carpets hanging from the walls, mainly depicting hunting scenes... You know, the carpets with dogs showing their fangs and deer and ducks bleeding from open wounds ... hunters wearing leather pants and hats with colorful pheasant feathers sticking up from them. At some point I passed through numerous sections dedicated exclusively to antique, robust furniture, all of it several centuries old. I came upon an old musical instruments section, too.

And then, the backbone of Western culture: religious art, an endless quantity of it -– mountains of it! An entire ocean of Crucifixions, of torn flesh, of deranged saints, of popes and cardinals ... benevolent, fatherly or frightening faces of God, perversion intertwined with gory images of hell. Soon I began to feel dizzy, confused and disoriented. I was not used to this shit anymore. I had been living in revolutionary South America – in a free country. This brutal mish-mash and dreck belonged to an absolutely different world, to a pre-revolutionary era. There was so much blood, so much suffering, so much fear, and no light and no apparent sign of even the slightest love for humanity. All the invented horrors, the Church and its rules, the torture and rape, in the name of something sacred ... all that gore for nothing but to shock and to frighten poor people, to force them into total submission. This is what has controlled the world for centuries! This is what violates my continent, robs its people of everything ... this so-called culture, so-called art, at the service of Christian fundamentalism and slavedrivers!"

Now there was deep silence surrounding Pablo Orozco. On this archipelago, religion was, well, sacred. The West and its allies had made sure of it. Wahhabi fundamentalism had been imported from the Gulf, Christian fundamentalism had been delivered direct from Europe and North America. Here, nobody dared to speak this way publicly. Religion was fatal, lethal, it could kill all before it, and had been killing hundreds, thousands, even millions.

"Why so much blood? Why so much fear, I wondered?" Orozco asked rhetorically, exhausted, dropping heavily onto an empty chair. He lay his forearms on the cracked dirty table and looked at the people who now averted their eyes from his.

"I felt terribly out of place," he said. "In all of that religious shit, I felt a clear and conscious threat and danger, an attempt to scare millions of poor human beings into absolute obedience, to make them horrified and defenseless. If this were really art, then to hell with it! It was not free at all, it was not even human! It served someone, it served something, but not humanity. Yes, it was so obvious that something significant and essential was missing in the halls I passed through. There was no warmth, no courage and absolutely no independent thought! Instead, I sensed the pathological narcissism and servility of the so-called artists, who had manufactured intimidating, idiotic and empty rubbish. And I thought: the enormous egos of these painters were evident to the naked eye, even through all the Gods flying around, through all the Christs hanging on the crosses! These works were drowned in the desire to please the church, the aristocracy, the monarchy and the military. The Louvre was mainly a tremendous intellectual bordello, or more precisely the greatest monument to the thousands of well-paid European and mainly male courtesans who had sold, through centuries, their talents and souls for cold cash and dubious status."

Mozart: Bravo!
Brecht: Yes, bravo! Neither of us could describe it better!
Mozart: And how true ... how true ... Us

too, in my day, in Vienna, Berlin...

'They don't understand anything,' thought Hans looking at his disciples – the present and future recipients of various European cultural scholarships and grants. 'They don't know what Orozco is talking about. Here he is, cutting to the essence, delivering one of the most damning indictments of European culture, and they don't comprehend. They perceive him to be an eccentric fool. They hear him as a crazy propagandist. They see him as a creature from a different planet, someone whom they will never follow and will never be able to understand. They are fully lacking in logical thinking, and they have not been encouraged to know and to compare cultures and ideas. They don't comprehend proportions and know nothing about ethics or history. They may flirt with ideas of revolution and social justice, they may wear T-shirts depicting profiles of Che Guevara, but offer them a car, a trip abroad, a scholarship in a foreign country, or even the latest model of a mobile phone, and all revolutionary zeal vanishes in a single moment. Orozco does not offer anything material, and that is why he can never win over a single local artist, a single intellectual, a single young man or woman here. Aurora is correct: this nation has been continuously robbed. Consequently, these people understand only the simplest language of survival – you give or you take, you rob or you get robbed. There is no quality of life in between. Orozco has not taking anything from anybody, but he is also not offering anything of financial value, and nothing instant. Therefore, for this crowd, for this country, he is irrelevant. He can tell them the truth, but they will not be interested or inspired by it. He can uncover crimes, and they will not be moved to action. He comes from a part of the world and from a culture, where some people put knowledge, truth, justice and love above everything else in life. These are the greatest treasures and virtues, the most breathtaking adventures imaginable. But not here. This is an extremely simple, brutal and practical world: You defend your own interests, now, right here, or you die. Orozco and the people here live on two different planets. Things have reached the point where Orozco and the locals cannot communicate about much of anything. And this is my fault, or more precisely, this is my greatest life achievement! We have made sure that people in almost all poor client states of the empire are not able to reason or to know anymore. They cannot create. They cannot think. They cannot live for particular principles. And thanks to religion for that. They are divorced from reality. They cannot be inspired. They do not even know love or justice. And they will never change! Therefore: we have finally succeeded. We won. We defeated communism!'

Mozart: Imagine, Genosse Brecht: I could see through that beast! I could read his thoughts. But there was absolutely nothing I could do to stop him.

"And then it hit me with all its force," Orozco banged the table with his fist: "Everything was stale there. There was nothing rebellious in the *Muséee du Louvre* or in all of Western culture! Nothing brave, nothing courageous, except for a few, proportionally negligible exceptions. Think about this: for all those centuries, Europe plundered the entire planet. Its palaces, theatres, universities and, later, train stations, tram lines, social halls, museums and research centers, public parks, hospitals – everything was built, literally, upon hundreds of millions of corpses of men, women and children of conquered nations. A monstrous plunder of your own archipelago paid for obnoxiously high living on the European continent. Yet, there was not a single renowned painter or sculptor who stood up and said: 'Enough, my fellow citizens! We are wrong. We are behaving like deranged beasts! Ours is a culture of brigands!' There was no serious demand to stop the slaughter and theft. In so-called Western art, I had a hard time finding even tiny signs of recognition that atrocious mass murder, extermination of entire cultures, and systematic pillaging were occurring in all the colonies. I saw no canvases depicting the horror of those who were slaughtered by the conquerors. No drawings accusing the colonizers of rape and torture. France exterminated entire nations and races on the Caribbean islands and in many other parts of the world. In some places, entire populations were slayed, but that was not even worth mentioning. Where were the brave European artists, the freethinkers? African slaves were dragged to North and South America by the British Empire, by the French, by the Portuguese and other Europeans. Millions died during ocean crossings. Again, the submissive hands of European painters and sculptors failed to record these details. There is hardly any description of all this in European literature – no one was ready to fight for these wrecked and enslaved human beings. Why? The answer is simple: because the citizens of Europe benefitted, as they continue to benefit to this very moment. Joseph Conrad's outrageously racist novel 'Heart of Darkness' is still held in extremely high esteem – one of a rare few, although unapologetic, testimonies to colonialism. French revolutionary art was created for the French people alone. The revolution fought to give rights and justice to French citizens, not to those who screamed in pain and horror under French colonial boots. 'Human zoos' existed all over Europe, filled with people from the occupied parts of the world. Captured 'natives' were locked in cages, in Paris and in many European cities, even in North America. They were kept naked and humiliated, exhibited like animals. French artists and thinkers never fought for non-whites. On the contrary! Go to the Military Museum in Paris – accomplished painters designed posters to attract curious crowds who wanted to see naked black bodies. Justice? What justice? For the people of imperial powers ... yes. But justice for the rest of the world, inhabited by ruined, tormented and enslaved human beings? What a farce! The Louvre is full of decorative art, intellectual whoring and laughable spinelessness. Europe was committing countless genocides, and its art remained shockingly provincial, complacent, cynical and compassionless. Of course there was a tiny minority with some conscience: Voltaire, Jules Vallès, a few others, tiny exceptions in an ocean of shamelessness."

*

'My trees and my dragons,' thought Aurora. 'What do they see from there, from above? What do they feel? Are they sad, are they in constant mourning over what has been done to this world?'

'It is all true,' thought Hans G, 'but what is really brilliant is that nobody gives a damn. Nobody notices it or writes about it! The population of this planet has been 'educated,' while others were re-educated, indoctrinated, conditioned and brainwashed by us – by the victorious and mighty Culture of the West. We can get away with all this – and we will! We always will... We can get away with even much more than this. Our values are the ones that really matter... What we say is the important thing. We commit crimes and then we judge others! Our measures are accepted as universal. Our judgments are never challenged. Our way of thinking is the only one that is allowed. We despise others, but we make sure that others admire us.'

Brecht: So well put. So true: We commit crimes and then we judge! Objectivity has lost its meaning. The terms 'good' and 'bad' are now determined by only one criterion: 'good' is all that serves the interests of the Western Empire; 'bad' is what challenges its global dictatorship. 'Good' is endorsed and 'bad' is destroyed.

Mozart: At least he is aware of the crimes that he is committing.

Brecht: Except he believes that his crimes are justified.

*

"It is not much different than what is happening right now." A delicate girl, of not more than twenty, approached Orozco. "In these days, colonized countries like this one are unable to birth incorruptible artists and thinkers willing to defend against imperialist onslaughts. Everything and everybody is for sale."

"You are right," Orozco replied, and then he smiled at her broadly. "The forms and practices of colonialism changed, but the essence is still there, in full force. And so is the shamelessness of local collaborators. It's the same as when those paintings I saw in the Louvre were created: still today, only a handful of white nations control the world. And go to London or Paris, Berlin or New York ... you will find almost no one who considers it significant, who fights for-"

"For what?" Asked Hans.

"For the majority of people who inhabit this planet," replied Orozco, giving him yet another mocking smile. "For the lives of the 'others,' for the 'un-people,' as George Orwell called them. And for a much better world!"

"Why would anyone fight for such things?" Hans said. "Look around. Look at the mess. Look at the magnitude. Look at where the money is."

"You fight," said the girl, looking straight at Pablo Orozco. "Tell him! You fight for the humiliated, robbed and injured human beings, for all of us. I saw your wonderful work on the Internet. I saw the brilliant work of your wife – Aurora."

"I do," Orozco replied. "We do. Aurora and I are fighting, and I would like to believe that we are actually winning. But I come from the Bolivarian Republic of Venezuela, not from Europe. "There are many artists in Venezuela and in Bolivia and in Cuba who are fighting for the oppressed people of our Planet. There are also many people like us in China. But our canvases are not hanging in the Louvre. Or in your capital city, or in this town, or in the commercial galleries of the empire, or on the walls of European culture centers."

"I think you should consider it an honor,"

smiled the girl.

"Who are you?" Hans turned to her with his well-practiced smile that could be interpreted as threatening, patronizing, and under some circumstances even encouraging. In reality, Hans was shocked. What was she saying? Where was this melody of the bygone years coming from? She was not supposed to say things like that. She was not supposed to think this way. She was supposed to listen to K-pop, she was supposed to patter constantly on her mobile phone, to communicate the frivolous via Instagram, Twitter, Snapchat, Facebook. She was supposed to Instafacetwit day and night. She was supposed to devour romantic comedies and horror films, to hum the same tune that everyone has been humming for decades. If she were an artist or a writer, all she had to do was to come to Hans, to beg for his grants and scholarships ... or join a civil society group or an NGO sponsored by the European Union or USAID. Above all, she should stay put and be quiet, instead of passing outrageous judgments and making political statements.

Aurora hit the table with a bottle of soda. She did it with the quick and powerful movement of her hand, releasing the bottle as it hit the table. The bottle bounced to the floor and broke into pieces. Everyone fell silent.

"Don't answer!" Aurora said sharply.

The girl stood up, and walked quickly toward her, and moved behind Aurora. She stood in her shadow, and even grabbed one of her arms in a childlike gesture. Intuitively and immediately, the enormous body of Orozco moved with unexpected velocity, and loomed over Hans.

Now the silence was complete. It began to rain. Heavy drops of water drummed on the sheet-metal roof.

Hans began to laugh. It was a theatrical and well trained laughter, very Central European and absolutely out of place in this tropical country known for its long silences and unfinished phrases. Hans himself had noticed that above all his laughter was panic-stricken, frightened and completely odd. He went on laughing while the rain fell relentlessly on the branches and leaves of the tropical trees and bushes, on the roof of the cafe, and on the surface of a small pond in the middle of the badly maintained garden.

The big dragon clouds had gone away, while the enormous branches of the trees remained.

Pablo Orozco moved to the girl and put his arm around her while she hung onto Aurora.

12

A Car Accident In Front Of The Cafe

*B*rakes squealing on wet asphalt, a car accident in front of the cafe, a single cracking sound, a fatal impact. Then there were no other sounds, except those of the rain. After a while a long, chilling scream... It was hard to say whether the voice – that outburst of pain, that simple expression of horror and desperation – belonged to a man or to a woman. It rose suddenly, resonated for several seconds, and then faded away. Silence returned again -– a deep tropical silence, all encompassing and exaggerated.

An old guard entered the café and simply announced: "She is dead."

Brecht: I don't understand...

Mozart: Someone trying to cross the street... Someone trying to escape the rain.

13

What Is The Purpose Of Real Art?

*O*ne of the local artists finally dared to address Orozco:

"What is the purpose of real art? What should art stand for? Whom should it serve? What should art do?"

"It should fight!" barked Orozco. He appeared to be shaken by something. Not by the accident outside, but by the intense behavior of his wife and this young woman whose shoulders he was still embracing. A few minutes after Aurora's scream, he continued to shield them.

"Fight what?" asked the artist.

"All that torments innocent and defenseless people ... people of any color, of any race, do you understand? Fight against corruption – especially moral rot. Art has to fight. It is obliged to fight against colonialism, imperialism and racism. And then... Fight for those who have no shelter, truly or metaphorically, and no certainty left in life. And especially fight for those who lost everything because of the greed of a few –– a few people or a few countries. They will tell you – the publishers, owners of the galleries, journalists, and even so many of your fellow artists – that such an approach is old-fashioned, that it will not 'sell.' They will tell you plenty of rubbish, but remember this: great art is only great when it serves other human beings, when it tells the truth and when it upholds the dignity of humankind. Art serves the people, or it is nothing more than an empty, decorative *papier-mâché*."

"To fight, one needs funding," said the artist, his face serious, even anxious. "How does one get grants or funding to fight against the torment of innocent people?"

"I need to get out!" Orozco turned to his wife. "Aurora, please let's leave immediately. I am suffocating. I am afraid I will begin to vomit."

Then he looked at the face of the young man. "If your brother or sister were attacked and savagely beaten, if they were about to be thrown off a cliff, would you fight to save their lives, or would you first look for a grant?"

Another artist – a girl –– stood up. Wearing her uniform black T-shirt, she too appeared almost indistinct from the others. "What about flowers and trees, what about beauty? Shouldn't artists paint beauty? Isn't describing beauty the most sacred mission of any artist?"

Orozco downed his mug of beer.

"Beauty is part of life and it should not be overlooked. But don't forget – the real artist is not a decorator – he or she doesn't struggle, doesn't suffer internally, doesn't go through a constant agony, merely to add a few colors to someone's living room. Once there was a painter – a tremendous Argentinean artist, and a good friend of mine – his name was Alberto Bruzzone. Someone asked him a very similar question that you are asking me now, about flowers and beauty. This was during the pro-Western *junta* dictatorship. Do you know Bruzzone's answer? 'I can't paint flowers or maternity when they are killing my students on the street.'"

"But nobody is killing students here, not right now," replied the artist. "At least not this year, I think."

"It was a metaphor," sighed Orozco.

"A metaphor?"

"And they are still killing them," added Aurora. "They are shooting at them, even as we speak. But they are not using bullets and mortars. Instead they are targeting and killing their brains, they are turning them into indoctrinated, emotionally and intellectually lifeless zombies."

14

A Young Artist Describes The Horrors Of Life In Her Country

"*W*hy are you so kind to me? Why are you protecting me?" asked the girl. Her features were delicate and simple, but her elegant white dress stood in stark contrast to the hapless uniformity of the clothes worn by the local crowd.

"Because you are similar to us," replied Aurora. "And because you remind me of my sister."

"Your sister?"

"She used to be inquisitive and full of doubts, like you. And she also used to be constantly frightened."

"What became of her?"

"She died. She was killed. One day I will tell

you more, maybe everything. But not now and not here... I cannot speak about it here. It is still too painful and too raw. When I think about what they did to my sister, I begin dreaming about revenge. I begin to hate. And when I hate, I always make disastrous errors. It is too dangerous to make errors in this country."

"I am so sorry. I should not have asked."

"Don't be sorry. It is always correct to ask. But now it is my turn to ask: why did you cry?"

"You saw? But my eyes were dry..."

"You cried."

"I did. Maybe I sensed your sorrow and I cried for her – for your sister. Maybe I cried for my country. And maybe I imagined what they would do to me if I remained."

"Remained where?"

"In this city. On these islands."

"You will not stay here."

"How could I not? Where would I go?"

"If you want, you can come with us, to Venezuela and then, maybe one day, to China."

"But..."

"There is no *but*! If you want to come with us, we will take you. Do you still have your passport? It was not stolen from you?"

"I have it."

"What about your family, your parents?"

"They would be against my going. My parents, my family -– they are like the rest of the people here. If they were to find out, they would try to stop me and prevent me from leaving."

"One more reason why you should come with us!"

"I know that. And I want to go... But can things happen so easily? Can change be so sudden?"

"Often, yes. Change can arrive unexpectedly and suddenly. Sometimes, it must. Pack your things while we wait in front of your house. We are leaving tomorrow. For tonight, we will get you a room in our hotel. In the morning the three of us will drive to the airport. Enough time wasted here. There is nothing we can change from within, at least for now."

"My passport is in my bag. I don't have to pack. I don't have many things, anyway. I'm afraid to go anywhere without the two of you, even to my house."

"From now on you don't have to. Once in Venezuela, I will teach you my art, if you wish. You are a painter, aren't you?"

"How did you know?

"From looking at your hands, and from the way you observe things. And from ... something else. Good then. I need a student and Pablo needs one, too. We never even had time to have our own children," she smiled. "Life was too full of breathtaking adventures, of fights, hard work and galloping from place to place ... and it still is like that."

"How can you be so kind and generous? You don't even know me."

Aurora waved her hand, dismissively: "We know you well. We are both artists. Can you be surprised that we might both have an extra set of senses? We know you and we also know what would likely happen to you if you were to remain here: you would be broken and forced to become like the rest of them. Slowly, you would turn to pretty frames with no real painting inside. You would be a proud whore, an unconscious prostitute of the system, a pretty plaything of its rulers.

"And what will happen in going with you?"

"You will become like us, if you dare!" Aurora laughed. "If you like what you see, then please join us. Otherwise, stay!"

"I've already decided. This seems more than what I could hope to ask from life. So, please take me, and please teach me, and help me clean all the accumulated poison from my body and soul. I may be a young woman, but I feel brittle and I ache all over. I can hardly recognize basic colors, or black from white. Sometimes I cannot differentiate truth from lies, and honesty from deceit. There is nothing I can trust."

They were still holding each other. Then Aurora spoke again:

"You are shaking. You are with us but you remain frightened. Tell me why? What are you so afraid of?"

"What is there not to be afraid of? What if all this is just a fantasy? What if I wake up tomorrow only to realize that this encounter never took place. I know that without you I am too weak. I would be lost, unable to resist. They are too mighty and their claws are everywhere. I don't want to become their new trophy, their conquest. I can still think, and I don't want to lose that ability. You know they break us here, if you don't believe in what they do, if you don't have a religion like them, if you don't indulge in the monstrous commercial pornography and emptiness of their family lives, even if you dare to ask a few simple questions... And people like him..." she waved her hand at Hans, "make sure we will never be able to escape, never break free."

"That much I know," said Aurora. "They do it everywhere -- in Africa and all over Asia. They tried it in Latin America as well, but there they failed, they were stopped, at least in several countries. They need all of you – and I mean absolutely all of you – to be converted into nihilists, into terrified and helpless beings who are constantly humiliated without even knowing that you are, and lacking the most essential self-respect. They buy and corrupt all those who are still capable of thinking and feeling independently. Those that they cannot buy, they liquidate. It is done now, and was done through centuries of colonial rule. Trust me, if it were up to them, there would be nothing pure and decent, nothing idealistic left on this planet. Everything would be only business and money, power and vassalage, control and slavery."

The girl nodded.

"Here they fully succeeded. There is not much one can do in our monstrously ugly cities: except pray and send text messages with no content between mobile phones. We drive our scooters and cars from one place to another, and we drive them at breakneck speed, but by the end of each journey we are confronted with the same void as at the start. Never in my life did I see a Russian or Chinese film – and I mean film, not a cheap soap opera. I had no idea how people think in other countries, what they fight for, and what they dream. Here they don't even tell us whether people on other continents believe in god, or whether they simply believe in justice. Our parents and grandparents are practically our proprietors. As with the rest of the people here, most of them are thieves and liars, but we are forced to respect and obey them, and this is how this awful society manages to survive intact. When we act against our will and throw ourselves at the feet of our perverse fathers, we call it love. In our families, we never discuss what is inside our souls and hearts. We do not mention our feelings and dreams, our fears and anxieties. That would be inappropriate. We only perform mechanical tasks of obedience and surrender. The emptiness inside our dwellings is a copy of the emptiness on the outside. And our families make sure that we don't become different, because if we were to succeed in living a full and meaningful life, that would be the most obvious proof of their own failure. In this country, there are several enormous cities, like horrendous sores. Each contains one or two million people with absolutely no culture and no theaters, no real art galleries or art cinemas, with only a few shopping centers and eateries where everything, local, Italian or even Japanese, has an almost identical flavor. Such cities have almost no public libraries, and if they do, there is nearly nothing thought-inspiring on their shelves. If, after many years of living here you are still a thinking human being, if you are not like them, like everyone else, if you managed by some miracle to maintain your sanity, your life is nothing short of hell, and there is no need to imagine and invent hell's agonies – hell is right here, it is all around you, squeezing you, crushing you, raping you day and night, night and day, for as long as you live. Your thoughts, your curiosity, your soul, and your dignity: everything gets violated, broken, contaminated, attacked. Until there is nothing left inside you anymore. Until you are no more... You eventually realize that it is better not to think, not to feel, not to rebel. Then you become exactly like everyone else, a zombie, an android. It is happening to all of us who are alive: you get beaten and shaped like wax into what they want you to become, day after day, hour after hour, second after second. You totally stop dreaming and imagining. Then there is absolutely no point in continuing to live... To stay, to feel their hands on my body and inside my soul, to experience the sharp, unbearable pain of being broken and reshaped by them, that is what I am so afraid of and that is why I am shaking."

"True hell is a country raped by colonialism," whispered Aurora. "To live in hell is to live in a country, in any country on this Planet, which has been crushed, violated and lobotomized by the West, by its lethal imperialism."

Mozart: I want to cry... I want to howl and cry. But above all, I want to compose: for that girl, and for her broken land.

Brecht: And of course, I want to write: day and night. From what she and Aurora have here expressed, one could draw inspiration for tens of powerful theatre plays, hundreds of novels and films!

15

Hans G Boasts About The Superiority Of Western Culture

"*I* was told about her. She is very stubborn, unpredictable, also fairly talented." Hans was addressing no one in particular, speaking about the young artist. "She should be exhibiting in the capital and then one day, who knows, even abroad."

"She is coming with us," said Orozco, looking straight at him.

"Coming with you? Coming where?"

"To Caracas."

"But why?" Hans shouted. He made a theatrical gesture, expressing absolute shock and revulsion. He waved his hands, trying to appear surprised, even shocked. His erection was gone, though his shirt was still soaking wet. "Why would you deprive this young talented woman of all the stunning beauty and inspiration surrounding her in this country? Why would you rob her of the staggering depth of her culture? How could you take her away from her family and friends?"

"Bad acting," smiled Orozco. "Second-rate stuff. Try harder, Hans. Give us a more convincing speech."

"What acting? I'm only concerned with this girl's future. She belongs here. This is a true paradise for any artist. Isn't this one of the most beautiful countries on earth?"

"It used to be," replied Aurora. "A long time ago it really used to be stunningly beautiful, but then the forests were logged out, the animals butchered, rivers and seas polluted and mountains converted into mining pits. Now garbage covers streets and alleyways in all the towns and cities. Filth floats on the surfaces of our waterways, and once merry streams and creeks have lost their voices, been poisoned and muzzled by chemicals and rubbish, and have lapsed into a coma."

"Hyperbolic!" Hans exclaimed, using his well-trained professional grin.

"Hardly. The emperor has no clothes, as in the fairytale. You are afraid that someone will say it, that someone will notice that there is hardly anything left of this country – that your empire stripped it naked and that what is left is a mere skeleton with a little bit of rotten flesh - – a decaying carcass."

"You hate this country. You hate your own

motherland." Hans always used this argument when everything else had failed.

"No! I hate those who made it like this. I hate those who made most of the countries around the world like this. I hate those who came from Europe and North America in order to plunder. And even more I hate those of my own people who submissively serve them, while becoming obnoxiously rich in the process. They deserve to be put in front of a firing squad, for committing treason. I am against the death penalty, but those who rob millions of their own people should expect no mercy. I also hate your political correctness: you turn my people into your butlers. You break their culture, even their identity, you kill their spirit, and then you embark on glorifying what is left – an empty shell without substance cast on the ground!"

Then Hans finally pronounced it:

"And you hate me."

Aurora did not hesitate for a single moment. She tossed at him, mercilessly: "Oh yes!"

"And you hate my culture."

"You probably know that Carl Jung did not mean only German fascism when he wrote, after the Second World War, that Western culture is nothing more than a pathology."

'She reads my mind,' he thought, suddenly paranoid. 'I was thinking about Jung not so long ago, and exactly about that quote, which Western academia has tried to minimize for decades.'

But instead he declared: *"You* hate my *culture.* Who cares about Jung?"

All that Hans was saying was a lie, a lie and a lie. His game was transparent and Aurora could easily see through it. Everybody could. Everybody who had paid any attention to this exchange.

"Am I the only one who hates your culture?" she replied. "Don't we all? Don't you as well?"

"Don't be ridiculous. How could I hate Beethoven and Schumann, and Mahler?"

Mozart: Let's check!

He dialed a long number on his mobile phone, drained his glass, and then shouted: Gustav, comrade... yes, this is Wolfgang here... in Chile, in Valparaiso... with Brecht. Yes, I am here with Brecht. Only one question: Gustav, do you hate Western culture?

A long unintelligible litany flew from the speaker.

Mozart: Thank you Gustav! Yes, I understand. All the best!

Brecht: What did he say?

Mozart: It's hard to repeat... plenty about mothers, about intercourse and rectums...

"Your culture violated Mahler," she said. "Your people forced him to denounce his Jewishness. He was not allowed to play in Vienna otherwise. After that, he lost his mind. Your culture ruined Mozart as well, along with so many others."

Mozart: She always thinks about us!

Hans could no longer bear it. He had been drinking for quite some time, at least seven bottles of a disgusting local beer by now. After all, this was one of the few places in the city where drinks were still readily available. Yes, he had been drinking and now he had had enough of everything, and he wanted to puke, and he wanted her – that woman with the local body but the posture and brain that belonged to an entirely different universe –– and the more he desired her, the more he knew that she would never be crushed under his body. So then he felt that it did not really matter – nothing mattered anymore. He felt humiliated and empty and unable to contain his wrath. He lost it, and he began to shout:

"So let me be frank with you, Aurora! Let me be frank, finally! Don't you see that Western culture is infinitely superior to all this!" he spread his arms, encompassing the entire café, the entire city, the country, the continent, and even the night. "How could anyone compare Wagner and Bach to the ... to the mediocrities – to the bunch of local pseudo artists and so-called intellectuals ... to those idiots? To the so-called dancers who jerk their legs and arms, in slow motion, while rolling their eyes in every direction like nitwits?"

Rain kept falling. Some people pretended not to hear, others simply did not understand. One of the artists burped loudly. Hans followed suit. He burped too, loudly and shamelessly. Lightning illuminated the group of trees that surrounded the place, as well as dozens of faces, and even the foam of the disgusting beer that had spilled on the table.

Aurora looked up and saw her dragons again, their mouths shut, their chins resting on several thick limbs of the trees. Their whiskers twitched. 'They come and go,' she thought, 'but they never really leave me.'

"Don't worry," Orozco doubled down and whispered into the girl's ear. "One day you will return and help your people take back what is theirs. We will all come back with you. By then, nobody will dare call you a pseudo-artist or an idiot."

"You made them like this," said Aurora. "You worked very hard to convert them into what you have described. But one day, the culture of these islands will return. And that will be the moment of judgment, as well as your end."

"Is Venezuela beautiful?" the girl suddenly asked Orozco.

"Yes, it is stunning. It has the highest waterfall in the world, a deep and impenetrable jungle, tropical islands and beaches, wide rivers, warm cities, plains and tall mountains. But it is not a perfect place as there is no perfect place anywhere on this Earth. We are building our country, changing it, trying to make it great for everybody. We work day and night, relentlessly. We call it 'the process.' *El processo*. We have millions of enemies, backstabbers as well as collaborators with the West. But we work our way forward.

She nodded. She wanted to understand. She knew she would understand one day, hopefully soon.

"I want to return, one day," she said loudly and clearly. "Riding on top of a tank, if necessary, in order to liberate this place. I want to rid this country of all the scum like you, Hans G."

Andre Vltchek

16

Wolfgang Amadeus Mozart Confronts Hans G And Western Culture

Mozart: And then I appeared, my dear Bertolt! I decided to become visible. After a few bottles of that repulsive local beer, I could not hold back any longer. I had to join in the fight. I felt obliged to confront that animal who was ruining millions of lives with my name on his lips.

Brecht: Good, my friend and comrade, Wolfgang! I have to say that it gives me great comfort to know that Hans G would never use my name when bragging about the Culture!

A man walked in. He seemed to be invisible to almost all the locals. Or at least nobody paid him any attention. A giant white wig crowned his head. The long sleeves of his shirt were made of lace, and his shoes were pointed, buckled and heeled.

Mozart strolled leisurely but determinately, straight toward Hans G. He grabbed an opened bottle of beer that was resting on a table, and took a large swig. Then he made a mocking grimace.

"What kind of shit are you drinking here?" he laughed. "Couldn't you at least teach them how to brew a decent beer? With all that fuss about our culture! You even consider rape to be part of it, so why not a good beer?"

"Who the hell are *you*?" shouted Hans, this time really petrified. His innermost thoughts had been wholly infiltrated.

He realized, or at least suspected, who this man approaching him was, and that if this spectre in front of him were truly Mozart's ghost, then he, Hans G, was endlessly fucked, indeed finished, and what was right now taking place around him was most likely the beginning of the final act, soon to be followed by his downfall and the final curtain.

"You know who I am," said Wolfgang Amadeus Mozart. "I am your culture. Ha! I am one of the regal symbols of that motherfucking culture that you and your cohorts are paid so splendidly to unleash against the rest of the world. In the name of my art and *culture* you and your barbarians are murdering millions of men, women and children in all the colonized countries of our Planet. Both Aurora and Pablo Orozco already told you that tonight. But let me add this: it is also the same culture that you have on the tip of your filthy tongue when you sodomize those poor women on the bed right in front of my appalled eyes. I am not speaking metaphorically, you monkey-goon-shithead-lackey-neo-post-Nazi trash!"

Hans' bowels began moving again –– only a warning but a significant one.

"Aren't you happy to see me, old mate?" screamed Mozart, making increasingly insulting grimaces at Hans.

"I don't believe in ghosts," said Hans.

"But here I am! A ghost of your great idol, your deity! How many lives have you ruined in the name of my art, of my *Kunst*?"

"Nobody else can see you."

"That's the way it was meant to be. Like the ghost of my father ... no one else could see him, no one else except me..."

"Much was said and written about you being haunted by your father's ghost, before you passed away," uttered Hans, for conversation's sake. From the bottom of his heart he damned the specter of Wolfgang Amadeus Mozart, for showing his image to him in this godforsaken place, for confronting him, for giving him such a fright.

Mozart interrupted him. He seemed to be in no mood for small talk.

"Stop cursing me! Don't you realize that I can easily read your mind? I came here to tell you something that you should never forget: the culture that you are glorifying and forcing on everybody ... You know, the culture that did all it could to starve me, to destroy me. It humiliated me, simply because I was different from the others and on top of it, exceptionally talented. At the end it succeeded. I went mad. I lived a very short and miserable life. In Vienna they treated me like an animal. For them, I was a trained monkey. But I managed to create *Don Giovanni*, the greatest opera ever composed. It was all about rebellion and courage and spite. My best work was like a huge nasty finger pointed at the sky, a finger shown to absolutely everything that was revered by them, by their establishment and their twisted religion ... a middle finger salute to the idiots in charge of the Empire and its pathetic culture, a kick in the ass to their priests and preachers. I did it in those toxic and bygone days, and if I were alive now, I would feel obliged to do the same thing all over again: to compose in order to confront 'the culture' and the Empire."

Mozart leaned on the table. He finished another beer, made a disgusted grimace and lit a clove cigarette.

"And I came to tell you one more thing, Hans G. All this stuff about our culture..."

"...Is shit?" interrupted Hans.

"Yes, and much worse than that."

"And you really think I don't know it, maestro?"

Mozart grabbed another bottle, opened it with his teeth and took a swig, then wiped white foam from his mouth.

"Back then, they weren't only starving me, they were starving many others, almost all of us. We were forced into shameless whoring. Me

... then comrade Mahler ... of course the Russian brothers like Tchaikovsky ... so many others ended up prostituting themselves, licking the hairy assholes and muddy boots of government officials, military officers, members of so-called elites and the church. Most of us, really..."

He emptied another beer and smashed the bottle against the wall. Then he burped, loudly.

"I have been listening closely. You could not see me, but I was here. And what is my conclusion? Pablo Orozco is absolutely correct. In my day, almost no one had the guts to rebel. And most of us were, as our counterparts are these days, nothing more than a bunch of self-centered megalomaniacs, who did not give a flying fuck about the rest of the world. And about those people who were killed by Europe across the continents? We never, for one second, thought about them! To us they did not exist, they were worse than the filthiest beasts! That's how our culture raised us. We could cry about an abandoned puppy or a kitten, but we would indifferently witness a murder of a fellow human being belonging to a different race, without even blinking an eye. We never dropped one tear for them, never composed anything about them. Face it! Do you think that brothers Liszt or Schubert thought about Arabs, Asians or Africans? Do you think that when our mighty comrade Beethoven composed his 9th Symphony he was dreaming about all members of the human race 'becoming brothers'? Of course not – he meant *us* – whites – Europeans, the only people, the only beings who possessed souls!"

Mozart was now sucking down other people's beer, taking full advantage of being invisible. He was getting pissed, slowly and gradually, one could almost say professionally.

"Do you think I have any good memories of Vienna? Do you know what I feel when I see this chap Orozco? I want to shout: 'If he had come to Vienna, or to Berlin or to Prague when I was alive, I would have joined him. I would have dropped everything and I would have joined him immediately!' Probably we all would have joined him. Then we would have composed, painted and written some absolutely different stuff! We would have created tremendous music: great revolutionary symphonies and operas, instead of all the religious clichés and rubbish composed in order to impress venal and syphilitic cardinals! All those odes and servile banalities were custom-made for the kings and emperors, for the aristocracy and for a few noble ladies. What a waste of our talents! If people like Orozco had been born several centuries ago, by now the world would be like nothing you could even imagine!"

"You call your own music crap?"

"Of course I do. Not all of it ... not all, of course. The best stuff that I composed came to me after I lost all hope and ideals, as well as dignity. That stuff was actually good. I suffered, I was starved, humiliated ... I composed from desperation. But can you imagine, with my talent, what I could have given humanity? If only I could have joined the revolution – if there had been a real revolution in my days! My music would break windows, and thick walls of palaces. It would help fire-up the people, bring them onto the streets, lead them to the barricades. It would break the chains on the hands and feet of African slaves. It would free the worker captives from the horrid mines in Latin America. My music would demand justice. It would attack degenerate rulers! It would inspire citizens to throw the damned preachers and priests from the windows! If only we had had a few decent people back then, a few people who could teach us how to think instead of how to expose our buttocks ... then maybe I would have been honored by becoming the people's composer!"

"But why? Why would you want to be like those worthless anti-social elements?"

"You mean, like Orozco? Watch out, you brigand! One more insult and I will smash your skull with this bottle full of piss. It's you and your damned governments who are anti-social. It is your own citizens who get fatter and fatter from booty and genocides. Watch your tongue, you scum! I knew and always hated the primitives, racists and morons like you. They were everywhere, surrounding me in Vienna and in Prague – I hated our elites, Hans G, our elites and the 'officials'! I hated their mediocrity, their stupidity, their egotism and pettiness. And those you serve now are even worse! They sacrifice millions of people without a single fart of compassion. They ruin entire nations to retain their tight control on the world. Deep inside, I am like Orozco, like Aurora, it's just that they were lucky to be born outside Europe, in a totally different era. Don't you know that all of us, at least most of us, the greatest of us, were all born with the desire to join a Revolution? That such desire has always burned in our hearts? We were destined to compose music, to write books and paint enormous canvases demanding racial equality, social justice, true power to the people, and above all the end of Western imperialism and colonialism. Instead we were castrated right after being born – castrated by the monstrous Christian religion, by our monarchies, by merchants and yes, by our 'culture'! We were conditioned, corrupted, brainwashed and frightened, not unlike these people here! All we were taught was how to compete, how to want more and more and more for ourselves and for our families: more and nobler horses, flashier carriages, prettier maids. We were taught that fame is actually the only thing that truly matters. We valued great applause in the opera houses and concert halls far above dignity and justice. It was always like this in Europe. It is the same now -– in the West and in all of its colonies. Greed and servility are what propel this so-called 'culture,' Hans G!"

'I want to shit!' thought Hans, desperately. 'I want to shit and puke and then run away.'

"Then shit and run with your trousers full of crap!" laughed Mozart. "But you cannot escape me and you cannot silence me, you idiot! I am a ghost. I am your fear, your worst nightmare! I will stick to you for as long as you live."

Hans felt very cold. He shivered, though the night was hot and humid, tropical.

"They bought us – they bought almost all of us – the most talented artists and thinkers were purchased like cattle. They addicted us to privilege, while the rest bled with envy, ready to do anything it took to join the chosen flock. The select few were elevated to fabulous heights, given villas and beautiful women, money, horses, coaches, butlers, chocolates, but above all, great respect and fame. In exchange for complicity, of course! They converted us into pathetic clowns and entertainers, into comedic whores, into pricey decorations, like chandeliers, into the trappings of sport, like rank hunting lodges, into irresistible triflings, trays of sweets at their galas. They did to us exactly what you and your gang now do to artists in the conquered world!"

"Why are you saying this, you horrible creature?" *Creature.* Hans caught himself using exactly the same insult invented for Mozart centuries ago by Antonio Salieri.

"I have been forced to watch you, Hans G. For years, I have watched you from above your own bed!"

Hans swore, and then swore again, and he did it in his native German language. He began to lose control over his mind and bowels.

"What I see in Venezuela..." began Mozart.

"What *you see in Venezuela*?" Hans

shouted at him. "How the fuck can you see *anything* in *Venezuela*? You never traveled to Venezuela. You never left our mother-fucking Central Europe! In your day, there were merely a few conquistadors, deranged priests and millions of native monkeys in Venezuela."

People in the cafe now observed Hans with horror. He seemed to be losing his marbles – he was shouting at the empty beer bottle, with an insane expression of hate and fear engraved on his face.

Then Mozart jumped on top of the tables, laughing, pointing at him.

"Monkeys! Now you show your true colors, you racist bastard! And don't play stupid. You know that's where we all reside now, most of the time. In Caracas, in Havana, La Paz, Quito, Rio de Janeiro ... and many of us moved to Beijing, and others to Hanoi. A few of us are working in Pyongyang, Johannesburg, in Tehran and Asmara. Who do you think is really coaching those legendary Youth Orchestras in Venezuela? And why do you think the Chinese musicians are now the greatest in the world?"

"So if you really are there in South America, you tell me: what the fuck do you see in damned Venezuela?" shouted Hans desperately, like a maniac, leaning on the table.

"I see real culture: engaged art, something we never experienced in Europe. I see Revolutionary art, compassionate art, provocative art. Art fighting for social justice. Art fighting against feudalism, racism, religious indoctrination and above all – against Western imperialism! I see real art and real culture!"

"Art can exist for art's sake," Hans mumbled, disoriented. "It can be pure. It should be pure..."

"It could be, but what is it worth then? It consists only of ego trips, of light pop melodies and colors stripped of any meaning; it is nothing more and nothing other than emptiness, self-glorification or self-pity, a medley of selfish private anxieties and hopes. Admit it: you know that art is the most powerful of human expressions and that is why people like you try to silence it, depoliticize it, to make it empty and irrelevant. Because you realize that art is also one of the mightiest weapons. It can inform, educate, and help to create a new world, and it can also smash to pieces the entire old and oppressive structures and dogmas!"

"Wagner would never..."

"A few weeks ago, Wagner told me personally that he would have loved to write music for Eisenstein's films. Instead it was Comrade Prokofiev who composed the music. Richard also confessed that he would have much rather composed grand operas about Simon Bolivar or Salvador Allende, than about Siegfried and his goddamned death."

"You are mad!" screamed Hans. "The entire world is going bananas."

"Literally, isn't it?" Mozart unloosed another mocking chuckle. "And stop swearing at and insulting us. Remember, we are your culture."

"My culture..."

"Another serious thing I would like to discuss with you: you should stop using our names and our legacy for your Machiavellian ends. Others sent me here to talk to you seriously – to you and to your brigand gang. We may all retaliate, terribly. You Must stop dirtying our names..."

"Or else what? What could you bloody ghosts do to me?" By now he was certain that they could do a lot. For instance, they could easily destroy him. That's what they were actually doing right now.

"We could go public. All of us. We have our ways. We could complain. Brother Shostakovich the other day threatened to approach RT, Granma, Prensa Latina and teleSUR if you don't stop disgracing him as an anti-Communist!"

Excited, the girl whispered to Aurora and Pablo Orozco: "Do you see him? There is Mozart's ghost chewing out Hans G."

Aurora nodded.

"How absolutely marvelous! Who else can see him?" asked the girl.

"Those who dare," replied Aurora. "Those who are truly alive."

"True," said Orozco. "We can see him, of course. In fact, he took this journey with us. Comrade Wolfgang Amadeus is our very good friend and a true supporter of the Bolivarian Revolution. We made him secretly an honorary member of several of our committees, and he is helping with the Youth Orchestras in several of our provinces. We did it covertly, of course, so nobody would accuse us of hiring ghosts. He doesn't like Caracas too much – spends most of his time in our smaller historic towns: Merida and Ciudad Bolivar. Chopin on the other hand is working in the capital – he's obsessed with the revolutionary murals at the metro stations, and with our new cable cars."

"And Victor Hugo is teaching creative writing in one of our former slums," said Aurora, proudly. "The students have no idea who he really is, but they absolutely adore his lectures."

Suddenly Mozart grabbed Hans by his shoulders and sighed:

"You don't really want to die being remembered as someone who lived all his life like a dirty worm, do you? Resign and do something decent! Go public with what they made you do for all these years. Write a book. Give an interview to RT, to Press TV or teleSUR. Do something similar to what John Perkins did years ago: write the '*Memoirs of a Cultural Hitman.*'"

The body of Hans G shook violently. He produced an unhealthy, loud roar and woke up. His head was resting on the table. It felt embarrassing. He was exhausted and unwell. Sticky sweat had spread over his entire body.

He did not feel any relief: he knew that although he appeared to have fallen sound asleep, what he had experienced was not really a dream.

Andre Vltchek

17

The Grand Finale. Religious Cadres Trash the Bar, Hans G Soils His Pants, Aurora Leaves, Hans Anticipates The Revolution, And He Falls

*W*hile Hans had stared at the table in an absolute stupor, ten men in long white robes entered the café. Their faces were covered, their hands clutched long metal poles.

"Who are these freaks?" asked Orozco. "They look like local replicas of the Ku Klux Klan."

"They are our religious zealots," replied the girl. "They attack bars and restaurants that sell alcohol. They are a self-appointed morality police. They are aided by the Gulf, by the most trusted allies of the West."

"What are they going to do?" Orozco appeared puzzled, even amused.

"They will trash the place."

"So these are your good friends and allies?" Now Orozco addressed Hans with unconcealed scorn. "Make sure they at least let us finish our beer, before they impose prohibition."

The men went to work with great proficiency and determination, something highly uncommon in this country. They first walked toward a small bar in the corner of the cafe, and began systematically dismantling it. All of its content, including bottles, glasses, mirrors, banners of Manchester United, and even shelves that held objects clearly unrelated to hell – clocks and black and white photographs of the city taken a few decades ago – were deliberately and thoroughly trashed.

"Are they going to burn this place down?" asked Orozco.

"It depends on their mood," replied the girl.

"So much wasted energy," sighed the great Venezuelan painter. "If only they would direct it at dismantling the feudal system or at building playgrounds for their children. Or at least they could try to free this country from Western influence, from its dogmas and market fundamentalism..."

"That's out of the question," explained the girl. "They can only build their own houses and places of worship. They cheat people out of their land. They are determinately against anything social or public. They would die defending capitalism. And they are thoroughly obsessed with money, exactly like the local Christians are."

At this point, Hans G. knew that his time had finally come: he had to go -– he had to shit, and he had to do it immediately. His bowels were moving intensely and loudly. But the hard-working white robed zealots were blocking the toilet and Hans guessed it would not be wise to disrupt their focused work and zeal.

"Any Israelis here?" screamed the tallest white robe, obviously their leader.

"Venezuelan!" replied Orozco.

"What's that?"

"Cheese," said Orozco. "Goat cheese."

"It's a country," said one of the artists. "But I can't remember where it is located, exactly."

"Where is your country?"

"Very near Qatar, *Alhamdulillah*," said Aurora.

"That's fine. Let him be. I noticed he looks like an Arab." Then to Orozco: "Stop drinking, you monkey! God is watching you." Then towards Hans: "What about that one?"

"Austrian," replied Hans.

"Australian devil!"

"Austrian," explained one of the local artists. "That's where Adolf Hitler came from."

"Oh, that one... That's fine then."

The white robes did their duty, rapidly and surgically. After all was neatly demolished, it was time to go, to enjoy a well-deserved rest.

"Stop drinking that shit, all of you, or you will burn in hell. One day you will come and thank us for our attempts to save you."

"It was terrible beer, anyway," commented

Orozco. "I was wondering whether these people were brewing it themselves to punish the *infidels*."

Mozart crawled out from under the table. "In my days, whoever brewed such piss would have been lynched by outraged citizens."

"You really are here!" shouted Hans in total despair.

"And where should I have been? My friends Pablo and Aurora are here. The three of us travelled together from Caracas. And together we leave."

The white-robed men formed ranks and began marching away. Hans watched them departing, suddenly realizing that for him it was too late. All hope had disappeared. He was too tired to fight. He was also too weak to prevent what was irreversibly coming: he felt as if all the terrible food he had eaten here for years was now trying to jet out, break his intestines, explode and kill him. It was fate! Fucking fate, as the Russians say... *Yobanaya sud'ba*!

Aurora, Orozco and the girl were ready to leave, too, and so was their friend Wolfgang Amadeus Mozart. Hans thought they all looked like gods – proud beings, in good spirits and full of confidence. The future was theirs. They were exceptionally talented and generous people. And among them was a local woman, still very young but also talented and bright -- a woman now embraced by them and rescued from his claws.

Then Rina walked in.

"*Sayang*! My love!" she screamed from the entrance. "I came to surprise you!"

Aurora stopped abruptly, as if remembering something. She turned around and went back towards Hans.

"I know a lot about you, Hans G. It was not you who violated and murdered my sister. If it were you, I would have killed you."

No pathos in her voice. Just stating what was obvious.

"I know that," he replied. "You would not hesitate, would you?"

"But because it was not you who terminated her life, it does not make you blameless. You ruined tens and hundreds of lives. Before I go, I have to tell you this ... in Spanish, because in English it somehow doesn't sound the same: *"Eres una mierda, Hans! Una mierda y nada mas."*

He understood Spanish, at least some, at least the basics. And these were definitely basics.

"You are a piece of shit, Hans G. A piece of shit, nothing else."

She repeated it in English, and then in her own language.

Now everybody was listening.

Slowly, unhurriedly, she pronounced the sentence in her native tongue, again and again, until it sank in, until everyone heard and clearly understood what she meant.

It stopped raining abruptly.

Then it happened. Or more precisely, it came out, with tremendous force and sound and it lifted him up from the seat for several seconds, while his eyes were still captured by hers. The rain was gone, the bar was demolished, and all that Hans G had painstakingly constructed for many years collapsed irreversibly in that very moment. It disintegrated, evaporated into thin air. His pride, his secure position in the universe – suddenly all gone.

He could not control his body anymore.

Hans G, director general of one of the enormous European cultural centers sponsored by the European Union, arguably the only *real* cultural center to speak of in the capital and therefore in the entire country, unexpectedly and shamelessly performed an earsplitting and terrible deed that would make the most humble peasant from the deepest local hamlet die of shame.

The act occurred while he was staring straight into the eyes of the most desirable woman he had ever met in his life – a woman he would sacrifice anything on earth to possess and to violate.

Then in response to the shame created by the lower part of his body, his mouth yielded a long howl of despair, a noise not unlike the beastly sounds made by huge Southeast Asian water buffalos.

Those powerful noises were soon followed by an unbearably potent stench.

Orozco did not even blink. He lit his Cuban cigar to neutralize the disgusting odor. He did it slowly. He was not really surprised: he knew that all snitches and secret agents of the Empire were by definition appallingly smelly.

Then they began walking towards the exit: Orozco, Aurora and the girl, their new comrade and student. Wolfgang Amadeus Mozart joined them, walking next to them, but only few people in the cafe could actually see him. Only a few people here were actually alive.

Before leaving, Aurora's face did not twitch, as if the stench had no effect on her, as if it did not surprise her at all. She turned around on her heel. She said nothing. She showed Hans G her back. She went with Orozco, her love. She moved on instinct.

'The entire great continent of South America is waiting, expecting Aurora and Orozco back,' thought Hans, with bitterness and envy. 'It's the continent that really matters now.' It was the continent that was changing the whole world, the continent pulsing with the wonderful and inextinguishable fire of the Revolution. It was the fire that he could never feel or understand, and which, therefore, he had tried to extinguish.

The continent bursting with creativity and pride was now expecting back its native son, his wife and comrade, and their adopted daughter.

Rina appeared next to Hans. She was not as refined as the others. She twisted her face in disgust, letting him know that she noticed, that she knew.

"You smell!" she declared loudly. Everybody could hear it.

"Go away, whore!" he shouted at her. "Go away or I will break all your bones, right here and right now!"

He despised her as much as she despised him.

"No you will not, you filthy pimp," she replied. "You filthy animal, you old stinky impotent goat."

'So you hate me, too,' he thought. 'Does everyone here, deep inside, hate me?'

Hans knew that he had lost. He knew that this very night, his culture had lost. It was defeated here, and one day it would be defeated everywhere else.

The future was clearly in Caracas and Quito, in La Paz, Santiago, Buenos Aires, Montevideo, Sao Paulo, and Havana. And of course, it was in Beijing, damn it!

A dragon lifted his head from the tree and slowly began levitating. Aurora did not know, although she suspected, that this tremendous creature of fable had never left her side since she had landed in this country. No matter the anti-dragon propaganda the West spread, dragons remained the wisest, kindest and most faithful beings on earth.

'I raped your sister! And when she was still alive I threw her under the wheels of a speeding truck!' He was going to scream these words at her back, at her slowly disappearing silhouette. It would have been a lie – he did not do it himself. He had spied on her, collecting information, but he did not commit the act itself. Others did, later. They did exactly that:

tied her hands to the pole and raped her, one by one. And then they caned her and burned her with cigarette butts. Finally, with one powerful blow of a metal bar, they broke her neck. She was five months pregnant. She was begging them to spare her life. But they killed her and threw her torn and battered body under a speeding truck. How on earth had it happened? How did things go out of control like that? Hans recalled every detail: he had offered her a grant and she refused. The grant was intended to stop her from producing her enormous canvases depicting Western powers corrupting local business elites, government officials and, yes, the artists. She had spat straight into his face. "You butler, you servant, you filth!" She had shouted at him. Then Hans denounced her to his superiors. They arranged the rest. She was kidnapped. She was raped, tortured and, finally, killed. Her body was disappeared.

If he shouted now into the darkness of the night: 'I raped your sister!' the lie would cost him his career and maybe even his life. But perhaps for him it would be better to be killed by Aurora or Orozco, than to lose her, than to have her disappear from his life irreversibly, in this most humiliating manner. Not because he loved her, but because he could not accept not being able to control her. An inability to control her meant that his power had clearly visible limits, and that one day soon it could vanish altogether.

For Hans and for the Culture that he was

paid to represent and promote, controlling the world was the main purpose of existence. He had never desired to control anyone as much as he had desired to control this woman who was slowly but determinedly walking toward her great destiny. Looking at her, he understood clearly that each of her movements was meant to insult and to humiliate him personally, as well as his values and his continent. She scorned him. She despised everything about him, from his pathologies to his mission on Earth.

'What China is to the West, Aurora is to me,' he thought. 'And this load of shit in my pants will never go away. I will have to carry it with me, no matter where I go. And then one more and much heavier pile of shit will haunt me as well – a huge pile that already contaminates my soul ... it will mark me for the rest of my life.'

Two piles of excrement prevented him from speaking, from getting up and running after her, from following his innermost instincts - from committing suicide. Subconsciously he knew that now, if he were to move, if he were to run after them, the two hard fists of Pablo Orozco would smash his face, mercilessly.

As rain resumed its monotonous drumming on the tin roof, Hans gazed after her, defeated, overwhelmed by melancholy and impotence. 'How grotesque were his values and his world to someone like her! he knew. Once again Hans recalled that Orozco was not much younger than he. Yet it was obvious that Orozco was all that Aurora longed for: Orozco the man, Orozco the artist, Orozco the revolutionary, Orozco and his legendary struggle, his longing for justice!

Sweating, shaking, trousers full of shit, Hans G felt that he had no place to hide, no place to escape. The dragons were against him. Kafka was most likely living in Quito. Mozart, Liszt, Mahler and Bartok – all in Caracas and La Paz, some in Beijing. The Russians had gone back to Russia: Shostakovich, Stravinsky, Rachmaninov and Scriabin. Schiller and Goethe, both were in Cuba writing odes for the Latin American revolutions under their new pseudonyms. Bertolt Brecht was shuttling between Beijing, Hanoi, Pyongyang and Latin America. They had all come back to life and they were now fighting against everything that he represented and promoted. His Culture, damn it!

'My reign may be ending, soon,' whispered Hans. 'This woman has refused me, and others may soon do the same. If they reject me, they may also reject this entire imposed culture, they may reject the dreadful values of their own twisted families, as well as their religions, even their own egocentrism -– the things that have been so painstakingly injected and promoted by me and by others like me, for decades.'

Brecht: He entered the cafe as a conqueror, as a trusted butler serving power. And he left like a dirty swine, exposed, defeated and totally alone!

Mozart: As he deserves! I hope you liked the story, my dear Bertolt. It is such a sad and dark tale, but admit: it has a really decent ending.

Brecht: The ending is the best. Goodness triumphs over evil! A beautiful story with excellently crafted characters. And you, Wolfgang Amadeus, played such an important and wonderful role. Let's order more wine, and celebrate.

Mozart: Let's! But before we do, let me confess that knowing more or less how this was going to end, I smuggled a Bose mini stereo into the cafe, connected my iPad and, before leaving, blasted my 'Requiem' at the highest volume.

Brecht: [laughing] Oh, you wicked you!

Mozart: But now let's drink. To the final victory and to the health of Aurora, Pablo and their rescued friend, their young comrade!

Brecht: Yes, let's drink to their health!

The centuries of conquest and plunder appeared to be ending – not with a war or global revolution, those had not erupted yet, but with a simple shrug of the slender shoulders of a passionate, brilliant and beautiful woman. They were ending with a scornful glance, and with the first step on a thousand *li* long road home to freedom.

The world was slowly awakening. It was preparing itself to face Empire, to confront Hans G, and to shave the heads of his whores.

Wolfgang Amadeus Mozart appeared in

front of Hans one more time. He was silent. Instead of words he raised his middle finger to the sky and looked straight into the eyes of Hans G.

Then the red flags began waving! Hans saw them. He saw people streaming toward the palaces and stock exchanges. They held banners. They were determined, strong and heroic.

A glimpse of the future ... And the music, tremendous, monumental and yet so human and kind, the music embraced the crowds charging against the old, oppressive regime. The music encouraged them, led them forward.

With horror, Hans recognized each and every great European composer behind this perfect harmony. Parts of Beethoven's 9th Symphony were there, too, but suddenly different, so different! "All men will be brothers!" roared the choir in Esperanto, not in German. The music levitated above the faces of all colors and races, above the peoples marching in revolutionary formations – ready for the final and decisive battle with Empire.

That was to come. That was the future that Hans managed to see, at least for a brief moment.

But now a very different music, loud and powerful, engulfed the entire filthy cafe. It came from nowhere but was suddenly everywhere: unstoppable, beautiful but also endlessly frightening, lethal. It fell on the place like a storm, like thunder, like fate. It was unmistakable: the *Requiem*. Mozart's *Requiem*

- the end!

'Aurora is beyond my reach. She is too beautiful for a man like me, she is Orozco's partner, she is brilliant, and she is free,' he thought, while falling eternally, in the moment before his heart stopped beating.

Epilogue

*T*wo days later, the building of the Cultural Institute in the capital city collapsed.

Several people living in the neighborhood testified that in the middle of the night, a tremendous roaring sound came from above and then from all directions. It was pointed towards the Center. The sound was deafening, but also euphoric. It was fatal. People confessed that they had never heard anything like it, before. First they were frightened, but then they felt goose bumps covering their bodies. They smiled and cried at the same time.

No one dared to go out. No one really saw anything. There was only that sound, and then the earth shook as the solid building collapsed and disintegrated into dust. Only two drunks, who were spending the night in the gutter by the Center, later testified that an enormous orchestra had besieged the place, arriving from who knows where. Male and female musicians were fully decked out, wearing local traditional attire, and the conductor stood on the highest step of the stairway leading to the main entrance of the Center. Three men stood next to him. One of the drunks, who when young had been a fairly talented local musician, swore that the group consisted of Wolfgang Amadeus Mozart, Ludwig Van Beethoven, and Gustav Mahler. The second drunk swore that the orchestra itself held at least five hundred members. "They played music, they played beautifully, but it felt like they were fighting a war, going into battle! It was as if they were settling scores with their own culture!"

Nobody took the two drunks seriously. But it was undeniable that by morning the Center was gone, and merely an enormous pile of dirt and dust remained where it once had stood.

2010 - 2016

Yokkaichi (Japan), Koh Lanta (Thailand), Beirut (Lebanon)

Aurora

About Author

*P*hilosopher, novelist, filmmaker, investigative journalist, poet, playwright, and photographer, Andre Vltchek is a revolutionary, internationalist and globetrotter. In all his work, he confronts Western imperialism and the Western regime imposed on the world.

He has covered dozens of war zones and conflicts from Iraq and Peru to Sri Lanka, Bosnia, Rwanda, Syria, DR Congo and Timor-Leste.

His latest books are *Exposing Lies of the Empire*, *Fighting Against Western Imperialism* and *On Western Terrorism* with Noam Chomsky.

Point of No Return is his major work of fiction, written in English. *Nalezeny* is his novel written in

Czech. Other works include a book of political non-fiction, *Western Terror: From Potosi to Baghdad* and *Indonesia: Archipelago of Fear,* also *Exile* (with Pramoedya Ananta Toer, and Rossie Indira) and *Oceania – Neocolonialism, Nukes & Bones.*

His plays are *'Ghosts of Valparaiso'* and *'Conversations with James'.*

He is a member of Advisory Committee of the BRussells Tribunal.

The investigative work of Andre Vltchek appears in countless publications worldwide.

Andre Vltchek has produced and directed several documentary films for the left-wing South American television network teleSUR. They deal with diverse topics, from Turkey/Syria to Okinawa, Kenya, Egypt and Indonesia, but all expose the effects of Western imperialism on the Planet. His feature documentary film *'Rwanda Gambit'* has been broadcasted by Press TV, and aims at reversing the official narrative on the 1994 genocide, as well as exposing the Rwandan and Ugandan plunder of DR Congo on behalf of Western imperialism. He produced the feature length documentary film about the Indonesian massacres of 1965 in *'Terlena – Breaking of The Nation'*, as well as in his film about the brutal Somali refugee camp, Dadaab, in Kenya: *'One Flew Over Dadaab'*. His Japanese crew filmed his lengthy discussion with Noam Chomsky on the state of the world, which is presently being made into a film.

He frequently speaks at revolutionary meetings, as well as at the principal universities worldwide.

He presently lives in Asia and the Middle East.

His website is http://andrevltchek.weebly.com/ And his Twitter is: @AndreVltchek

Aurora

"*A*urora is a tremendous work. Aurora is what a literary work should be: fully human. It is also what used to be known as a major literary work because it's rare to its time. It represents a leading edge of consciousness, courage, and social need. A major work! That's why it must be buried, as we know. I'm glad I can be part of it. Aurora is written at a consistently intense, dynamic level. I wish it could be 500 pages and dropped like a sonic boom on all the acclaimed literary centers of the world and be released like a climatic change for the good in the rest of the world.

Perhaps the most vital feature or effect of Aurora is that it expands consciousness, or perception. It thinks the unthinkable: the bankruptcy and worse of The Louvre, etc, the culture. It does what a lot of great works of art do: it criticizes art itself, explicitly and implicitly, and in doing so helps to make the needed room for itself, in the world of art and in the world in general. It creates and helps generate new thought, understanding, perception going forward. It helps not only express the full human condition; it helps transform it. It's a working work of art, a badly needed new experience. It enters the battle. It will be ignored, dismissed, and fought by the old world, while by the new world it will be part of another story entirely."

~ *Tony Christini*
Author of *Homefront*

*"T*errific!

Andre Vltchek's marvelous novel, Aurora, is one of those small books whose impact far exceeds its length. It is a highly polemical book in some ways, but also a fantastic journey of the imagination. Comparisons could include Juan Rulfo's Pedro Paramo, and Rene Daumal's Mount Analogue; but also Bulgakov and Leonov, Borges and Upton Sinclair. It is part Utopian vision, part nightmare, and part simply a vastly original inspiration. Like all works of true originality, it is, finally impossible to define, but it is possible to read it, and so you should, as quickly as possible."

~ *John Steppling*
Playwright, screenwriter, and philosopher

*"S*tarting into Aurora's political speeches -– this is up there with Camus' The Fall, Sartre's Nausea, philosophical novels that come to my mind – a different philosophy expressed of course – but of that caliber!

It is a beautifully written examination of our plight, a call for justice and action, an exact description of capitalism and its horrors and the hope that is socialism.

The use of Brecht and Mozart as a Greek Chorus works very well, I was not sure it would but it does. And they provided necessary comic relief at points where the reality became unbearable for a moment and carried the story forward with humor, biting satire, wit, and allowed us to step back and watch what they are watching.

The character of Hans G, to stand in for capitalism and imperialism, is made a more than cardboard cutout figure -– he is someone who can't see, does not want to see, what he is – but he is forced by Aurora and the others to face the facts of what he has done and what could be.

It is a beautiful and powerful piece of writing. Vltchek makes his points but escapes being preachy. I would call it a philosophical novel, using a scenario to raise the consciousness of the reader. But it could also be a powerful piece of theatre. The whole thing could be staged and acted out word for word.

No one writes like this anymore."

~ *Christopher Black*
International lawyer, writer, poet

"*W*ritten by one of the greatest living communist revolutionaries, intellectuals, writers, philosophers, artists and travelers that I know, Aurora is the best novel published recently that I have read. It is certainly a must read for all people struggling for liberation from capitalism, neo-colonialism, and imperialism and from the decadent, brutal, barbaric Western culture that continues to cause so much pain and destruction of the freedom and humanity of not only the 'Third World' countries but also the Western countries as well.

Through a focal character in the novel, Hans G,

the author provides the most glaring exposure and description of the functioning of the present-day system of neo-colonialism in relation to the past and present history of Indonesia in particular and the 'Third World' including Kenya and Africa in general.

Not only is Western imperialism decaying and rotten but it is actually rapidly being resisted and brought down by revolutions in 'Third World' countries such as those in Latin America led by communist revolutionaries represented in the novel by Aurora and Pablo Orozco. Thus Aurora ends optimistically — that capitalism and imperialism will be defeated and socialism and communism will ultimately triumph.

Yes, Aurora should be a handbook to all persons who are struggling for a new world order in which all human beings live as human beings and treat each other as such...."

~ Mwandawiro Mghanga
Chairperson, Social Democratic Party, Kenya

Aurora

POINT OF NO RETURN

Point of No Return shows the world through the eyes of a war correspondence, visiting places that are rarely covered by the mainstream media, offering provocative points of view about the pitiful state of today's world, its disparities and scandalous post-colonial arrangement – including global market fundamentalism and neo-conservative culture that are overthrowing democratic principals that humanity has fought for over centuries.

"André Vltchek is a writer, the real thing, of the same caliber and breed as Hemingway and Malraux."
                                        - Catherine Merveilleux

"Andre Vltchek tells us about a world that few know, even when they think they do. That is because he tells the truth, vividly, with a keen sense of history, and with a perceptive eye that sees past surfaces to reality..."
                                        – Noam Chomsky

"Point of No Return is one of the great novels of the 21st century. It deserves a wide readership and serious critical appraisal. Over a half century ago, in his important book "American Moderns - From Rebellion to Conformity," the great literary critic Maxwell Geismar noted "Our best literary work has come from writers who are outside [the dominant] intellectual orbit, where [capitalist] panic has slowly subsided into inertia."

Geismar anticipates Vltchek. Point of No Return explodes from that vital realm far beyond hegemonic control."

– Tony Christini, author of *Homefront*

"Point of No Return is riveting."

- Paulin Cesari, *Le Figaro*

"A fascinating look at the world through the eyes of a war correspondent – a world few of us know."

- Eve Jackson, *France24*

"Once again, it's the context that makes the book. It is quite simply mind-boggling. Andre Vltchek knows very well what he's talking about (...). It is a book that cannot fail to move, a rich, strong and dense tale, by all means get a hold of a copy for an intelligent read!"

- Yves Mabon

"Quite simply a masterpiece... All of the absurdity of our society, its lack of humanity and sense blows up in our face... All readers will feel touched by this narrative that speaks of liberty, choice and our place in the world."

- Stephanie Morelli

"A splendid novel that will leave no one cold. The author skilfully takes us along on a mysterious and sorrowful journey. A gripping read. "

- Patrick Martinez - *Radio Coteaux*

"André Vltchek offers an unsparing portrait of the world we live in. With his provocative outlook, he lays bare a situation that is really quite simple, and did not begin yesterday... Although this book does not raise easy questions, it is indeed easy to read, thanks to the wit and subtlety of its author. "

- Françoise Bachelet

"Andre Vltchek's work has the incredible capacity of helping one break free from the culture of denial. His ability to translate reality into fiction is stunningly original and very personal. His work shocks you while at the same time reconnect you with the political realities of today. Wisdom can only from a clear understanding of the past and some brutal honesty. This is the purpose of Andre's political novels."

- Anuradha Mittal, *The Oakland Institute*

"... despite all the terror and despite somber analyses about the battle between "market fundamentalists and religious fundamentalists" being the main contradiction of our time, Vltchek's novel projects the same desperate hope that once emanated from *Man's Fate* by André Malraux or *To Whom the Bells Toll* by Ernest Hemingway ... And as a matter of fact, Vltchek evokes strong memories of them, but not just because of his reawakening of the buried tradition of political fiction, but also because of his immense narrative talent ... Just like authors as Dan Chodorokoff, Ron Jacob, and others, Andre Vltchek is turning another chapter in the history of American literature."

– Michael Schiffmann

Aurora

EXPOSING LIES OF THE EMPIRE

Exposing Lies of The Empire is perhaps the most complete, and the most comprehensive account of the last several years, during which our planet has risen up and began its struggle against the Empire and its oppression. Vltchek takes us to all the continents, to slums and palaces, to the villages bombed into the ground, and to the front lines of the revolution. It alerts and provokes, clarifies and leads forward. It is a book of philosophy, a collection of exceptional investigative journalist reports, and a manifesto. It will inspire millions. It will be quoted for centuries to come.

"In an age of formula media, Andre Vltchek's work is truly exceptional -- fiercely independent and bracing in its challenges to the echoes and lies of the great power."
- John Pilger

"Brave international correspondent and author Andre Vltchek has written countless essays and many books on the problems afflicting the world, from social injustice writ large, hidden institutionalized brutality, super-power hubris, and ecological murder, to the hypocrisy of entire cultures, beginning with the "Atlanticist civili-zation" that currently decimates the planet implementing the agendas of Washington's insatiable Neocons and a savage, cynical capitalism. Naturally, all of this is done in the name of those two sacred cows of all US world interventions: freedom and democracy...

This is one of Vltchek's most useful volumes, an

anthology packed with the indispensable facts, first-hand knowledge, mature reflections, and righteous revolutionary furor necessary to combat the imperialist beast in all latitudes."

- Patrice Greanville, *The Greanville Post*

"Exposing Lies of the Empire is a monumental work.

...the modus operandi of Andre Vltchek: go to the region, discover with purpose, and interview people from all walks of life to get the fullest possible local views, Weltanschauung, and insightful commentary on disparity along the power continuum.

... His reportages are about casting light on the ravages of western militarism and western rapacious capitalism for the rest of the world, pulling on the heart strings of the relatively comfortable people in the West...

In this book, readers can discover through Vltchek's words and photographs what life is like for the peoples embattled by insouciant capitalism in far-flung places: to name a few — Syria, Eritrea, China, North Korea, Venezuela, Palestine, Viet Nam, and exotic locales few will have heard of, such as Kiribati.

Vltchek does not hold back as to what is harming people in the non-western lands. He points his finger — backed by evidence and compelling reasoning — at capitalists; capitalist's bloody henchmen, the military; empire's putschists and torturers; economic hitmen; collaborators; religious dogmatists; racists; the education (sic) system; media disinformation and propaganda; etc.

This is a book for everyone. Get it, read it, and become an informed citizen of earth. Find out what our broth- ers and sisters are resisting and solidarize with them. In particular, people who work within corporate journalism should read Exposing Lies of the Empire and find out what an authentic journalist really does."

– Kim Petersen, *Dissident Voice*

Andre Vltchek

Aurora